Frank Brownlee (1875-1952) was the seventh son of parents of Scottish missionary stock associated with the Transkei Territories. His grandfather, the Xhosa linguist John Brownlee, had arrived in 1816 and founded King William's Town. He was born in Cape Town where his father, the Hon. Charles Pacalt Brownlee, CMG, was the Secretary for Native Affairs of the first Administration under Responsible Government of the Cape of Good Hope. Young Frank grew up among writers, as both his father and his mother Frances, as well as his elder brother William, were to leave accounts of the frontier events they witnessed.

Educated at Dale College and at the Lovedale Institution, he entered the Department of Justice of the Cape Civil Service in 1893, served with the British forces at the Battle of Paardeberg (1900) and became the Railway Protector of Natives in 1903. During World War One he was appointed the military governor of Grootfontein in the former German colony of South West Africa, from which he began publishing articles in anthropological and historical journals. He married Susanna Hobson and in turn had several sons. Following the family tradition, he also held magistrate's posts in Eastern Cape towns, compiling the *Historical Records of the Transkeian Native Territories* in 1923. Thereafter, while resident in Butterworth – one of twenty-seven magisterial districts, of 260 square miles in extent with a population of 25 000 – he began collecting oral histories. In 1934 he was appointed to Pretoria as the Union's President of the Native Appeal Court. With his retirement in 1935 he contributed prolifically to the local press, and placed many stories overseas as well, in publications such as *Chambers's Journal*. He also encouraged other writers, for instance in 1935 contributing a preface to H I E Dhlomo's play about the Cattle Killing episode, *The Girl who Killed to Save*, which features his own parents as characters.

His first novel was published by Jonathan Cape in London as *Ntsukumbini* (1929) and reissued in the Life and Letters Series under the new title *Cattle Thief* (in 1932 and thereafter). *Corporal Wanzi*, his collection of stories, appeared in 1937, with many of them becoming anthology favourites, while his gathering of 'Native Folk Tales from South Africa', *Lion and Jackal* (1938), also went into several impressions. His last long work, the novella *Chats with Christina*, was completed shortly after World War Two. Dealing with the period of his father's term as Chief Magistrate of East Griqualand (from 1878 to 1884), it has not previously been published.

Ethelreda Lewis, from a projected foreword (1928):
'*Cattle Thief* is a book written by a man who has been in and out of the kraals from childhood and who speaks the language of his black friends with full knowledge and respect. Its literary quality will endear it to the fastidious reader, no less than to the admirer of a vanishing native simplicity and dignity.'

Everyman, London (January 1930):
'The speaker is an old black man who recalls his adventurous life episode by episode. Once the reader is accustomed to the use of the conventional white man's idiom and technique by an African native, the story holds one with its directness and dramatic power.'

The Sunday Times, Johannesburg (May 1930):
'Most people who know Africa can't write and those who can don't know the country and display the fact at every sentence. Frank Brownlee, as *Sunday Times* readers will know from his occasional contributions, has a flexible, good and expressive style.'

Dora Taylor in *Trek* (July 1942):
'Frank Brownlee is a fatherly representative of black trusteeship and his novel, *Cattle Thief*, is a series of conversations and revelations on the part of an old African, who is depicted as a fine, brave, cunning, courteous and extremely loyal fellow, and who certainly knows how to flatter his white "chief". Written in a charming style that captures something of the colourfulness of primitive speech.'

CATTLE THIEF

Frank Brownlee

PENGUIN BOOKS

PENGUIN BOOKS

Published by the Penguin Group
Penguin Books Ltd, 80 Strand, London WC2R 0RL, England
Penguin Group (USA) Inc, 375 Hudson Street, New York, New York 10014,
USA
Penguin Group (Canada), 90 Eglinton Avenue East, Suite 700, Toronto,
Ontario, Canada M4P 2Y3 (a division of Pearson Penguin Canada Inc)
Penguin Ireland, 25 St Stephen's Green, Dublin 2, Ireland (a division of
Penguin Books Ltd)
Penguin Group (Australia), 250 Camberwell Road, Camberwell, Victoria 3124,
Australia (a division of Pearson Australia Group Pty Ltd)
Penguin Books India Pvt Ltd, 11 Community Centre, Panchsheel Park,
New Delhi – 110 017, India
Penguin Group (NZ), Cnr Rosedale and Airborne Roads, Albany, Auckland
1310, New Zealand (a division of Pearson New Zealand Ltd)
Penguin Books (South Africa) (Pty) Ltd, 24 Sturdee Avenue, Rosebank,
Johannesburg 2196, South Africa

Penguin Books (South Africa) (Pty) Ltd, Registered Offices:
24 Sturdee Avenue, Rosebank, Johannesburg 2196, South Africa

www.penguinbooks.co.za

Cattle Thief, first published as *Ntsukumbini* 1929
This edition of *Cattle Thief* with *Chats with Christina* published by
Penguin Books (South Africa) (Pty) Ltd 2007

This edition copyright © Stephen Gray 2007

ISBN 978-0-143-18554-3

Typeset by CJH Design in 10 on 12.5 pt Palatino
Cover design: African Icons
Printed and bound by Paarl Print, Cape Town

Contents

Frank Brownlee in frontier days
(courtesy of the National English Literary Museum)

Preface

Had this book been written for South African readers only a preface would not be necessary, but it has been intimated to me that there may be many who will want to know who Ntsukumbini was, where he lived, how I came to know him and how I came to write his story.

When one has lived for many years among South African natives, attended their marriage celebrations, hunted with them, spent nights in their huts and been initiated by them into blood brotherhood, one becomes acquainted with intimate facts concerning them which do not come to the knowledge of the casual observer.

In my capacity as Native Commissioner the study of native mentality has appealed to me not only as part of my job but also as something intriguing in its ingenuousness and fascinating for its subtle simplicity.

Hours spent in native huts, where the warmth of the smoking fire has been shared with the inmates by dogs, cats, fowls and goats, have not been wasted – knowledge was always to be gained there. The head of the kraal would explain in detail the inwardness of some obscure custom, or he would recite some fable that had been handed down from ancient times, or he would give a graphic description of some historical event redounding to the credit of his chief or tribe.

With a knowledge gained in these or similar circumstances

and surroundings the writing of Ntsukumbini's story became possible.

It must not be concluded that most South African natives are thieves. Far from it. The average 'red' or raw native is inherently honest, but there have been certain families and clans with whom cattle-lifting has been a traditional profession. To such a family Ntsukumbini belonged.

There was something sporting in the way these people carried out their operations. The poor, as a rule, were not robbed; toll was taken from the fat herds of the rich. I have reason to know that thefts were sometimes carried out merely for the purpose of demonstrating skill in stealing, this in particular when it came to the question of initiating a new and youthful member into a society of thieves.

Ntsukumbini lived in the Transkeian Native Territory, a native reserve lying southward of Natal, bounded to the westward by the Drakensberg Mountains and eastward by the Indian Ocean.

This reserve has an area of 16 000 square miles, with a diverse native population, mostly barbarian, just short of a million. It is governed by a handful of officials and police. It is the finest part of South Africa, well grassed and wooded and watered. Here the native may, if he wishes, live a tribal life, but he is encouraged by precept and example to adopt European methods in husbandry and in his mode of life generally.

The Native Commissioner who hears his cases does so not only as a Magistrate but also as a native chief, taking cognisance primarily of the native custom surrounding the matters at issue, at the same time applying to them the principles of British equity, justice and fair play. Education is put within his easy reach mainly by the agency of missionaries, who have laboured here for over a century.

Ntsukumbini belonged to a tribe called Amaxesibe, which

about two centuries ago migrated southward from the country we now know as Natal. He lived on the banks of the Umzintlanga River at the foot of a high rocky koppie. His homestead consisted of four round thatched huts with a large cattle-fold. The kraal is surrounded and almost hidden by mimosa trees. On the rocky heights above stately aloes grow. From the vantage point of the koppie's crest Ntsukumbini could observe the country for many miles about and keep a watch on the approach of inquisitive people who might wish to interfere with his business. It was here in his declining years that he related to me the experiences recorded in the following pages.

The Amaxesibe are a fine people, tall, upstanding, deep-chested. Though peace-loving, circumstances made them war-like. They were from time to time threatened with extermination by stronger tribes, but their courage and determination enabled them to retain their tribal entity.

Ntsukumbini is a typical Xesibe. In the prime of his manhood he must have been of herculean size and strength. Even in his latter days, when I knew him at the age of about seventy, in moments of excitement traces of his former vigour would show themselves.

Kindly reader, deal patiently with Ntsukumbini. His mind does not work in the same way as your own. You go direct to a point, he reaches the same neighbourhood, but by devious ways.

Those who are acquainted with South Africa will realise that this story does not pretend to be accurate in its geography. Names of places and localities have been made use of other than those which actually formed the scenes of the several episodes.

My good friends Madevu and Skwenene the Traders may see that I have taken a liberty in the use of their Xhosa names.

They will know that these have been substituted for those of the storekeepers with whom Ntsukumbini had dealings.

Jack, Jim and Rooi Piet may or may not recognise themselves. The two former, I know, will not mind my having recorded the part they played in Ntsukumbini's affairs. As for Rooi Piet, if he feels himself to have been sufficiently identified to warrant his bringing a libel action, why, let him get on with it.

Dumezweni, the Magistrate, has been dead these many years. What has been said of him 'will not harm him in the place to which he has gone'.

The author with one of his Xhosa headman informants in the 1920s

1

Youthful Days

Chief of mine! It is kind of you to come and talk to an old man such as I am. My head is grey, my eyes are dim and my back is bent, but when I speak to you of the old days I feel for the moment young again. Most of my old associates are dead and gone, and many of the white men who knew me have also departed, so there is now no reason why I should not speak freely. What I may say is not likely to harm them in the place to which they have gone.

You say you intend to write down my words and put them in a book. What have I to do with writings and books?

As a lad I went to school for a year or two. I even learned to read a little: 'Ned is in the pit', 'Fat cats sit on mats and nod at men', 'Can a ram sit on a sod?' and so on. I remember these things well because I learned them with great pains, but to me it all seemed foolishness. Even a small child just learning to talk could tell you that a ram is not able to sit on a sod! So I say what have I to do with books or writings? But stay, I did have something to do with writing. As I learned to read a little so I learned to write a little, and I made good use of writing years later. But, my Chief, everything must be set down in order.

My teacher said I was dull at learning and beat me. I resented this and thought how I might humiliate him. I knotted the grass across the path leading to his hut. When he tripped over the knotted grass and fell into the mud with his new trousers on I was satisfied, but he was not. He found out that I had done that thing and had me dismissed from the school.

I was by this time big enough to herd cattle. My father put me to that work. I liked it because it meant being in the open veld all day; moreover, it was easy to avoid the work and leave the cattle to their own devices while I and my companions went to a pool we knew of and bathed, or made oxen of clay or hunted birds. I liked the work of herding cattle.

One thing I noticed in my new occupation was that every now and then fresh cattle would appear with our herd and others that we had known for some time would disappear. This puzzled me. It was not seemly that I, a youth, should question my father about matters of this kind, so I decided to find out for myself. I had noticed that it was always in the very early mornings that our herd was so many more or so many less. Enlightenment came upon me gradually.

On a certain day a man with attendants came to my father saying that one of them had missed a red cow with a white back. They wanted to know if by any chance such a cow had been seen near our kraal. I knew that a cow like this had recently appeared with our cattle. What surprised me was that my father should deny all knowledge of a beast of this description, whereas he well knew that there was such a cow with ours. The men insisted that the spoor of this animal had been traced to near our kraal.

My father denied all knowledge of a stray animal or its spoor and, protesting, called me, his herd, to bear witness as to the truth of what he said (he had told me what to say): We had no such cow, never had had such a cow and had never seen or heard of such a cow. My father said: 'You hear what my herd says. He is the one who knows the cattle even better than I do myself.' I knew the cow well. We had given her the

6

name of Rooimuis, but having testified before the men that we knew of no such cow I realised that it would be unfitting that she should be found with our herd, so being released by the men from cross-examination, I hastened to the hillside where the cattle were grazing some distance away, out of sight of our kraal, and quickly drove Rooimuis into the midst of a neighbouring forest, where I knew she would be content to remain browsing on the soft grass.

I had hardly returned to the kraal when the men in search of their missing cow emerged from the hut in which they had been sitting while questioning my father. I heard my father say in a loud voice while he kept one eye upon me: 'Oh, men! Come and examine my herd, and if you find the beast you have lost or one even remotely resembling it I will hand the beast over to you and will add two to it, so that there may be peace and good fellowship between your people and mine.'

Those men went to the cattle where they were grazing. They inspected the herd and found no beast such as the one they had described, so complimenting my father upon the sleekness and good appearance of his cattle and with apologies for their intrusion they proposed to withdraw, which my father would not permit them to do till they had partaken copiously of his beer.

My father killed a goat that night. Of the meat I received a liberal portion. I sat near the fire grilling bits on the coals. I had a knife which I had bought for a tickey at the store of a neighbouring trader. On its handle was written 'TRYME'. I always wondered what 'tryme' meant. I supposed it to be some kind of takata (witchcraft) word of the white people. With my knife I ate meat like the men. Directly I saw a piece sufficiently grilled I took it off the coals, held one end in my hand and gripped the other with my teeth, while I sliced off a piece with 'tryme'.

It was while I was paying more attention to chewing than anything else that I realised my father was talking to the people who were in the hut and that he was talking at me. I listened. 'Yes,' said my father, 'cattle are our life. One man has many, another has few or none. The men of our clan have always thought that if cattle were equally divided everyone would have sufficient. So it has been the custom of our people to take from the herds of the wealthy and add to the cattle of the poor. If by chance we have now and then kept an odd beast for ourselves, has it not been earned in a good cause?'

I see, Chief, that you become restless when I speak to you openly of our methods and our ways. There is that between us which prompts plain speech. You having been accepted as one of our clan, what is there that we should keep secret from you? I do not tell you these things as to a white man; I speak to you as to a Chief of our people. I know that you have much business in administering the laws that the white people make for us. It must take up much of your time to see that the Government laws do not press too heavily upon us. It is for us not to be found out when we break them. We are a simple people, and in observing our own customs we sometimes find that we have broken laws of which we know nothing. We know that you will deal gently with us when you find us in error.

I have told you something, Chief, of my youthful days. There is no need for me to waste your time with the small affairs of children, but I must tell you that I was given my name at the time of my birth and I have been called by that name ever since. The people said that when I was born my mother was in labour two days, a thing unusual with our women. The men said, 'Ntsukumbini!' (two days) and that is how I received my name. My father's name does not matter. In any case, as it is hlonipa (taboo) to me, it is not seemly that I should mention it.

8

There is a man without who is importunate in his demands to see me in regard to a matter of trespass of cattle. He is a common fellow and may wait while we converse, but if you feel that you would not hear what he has to say, as the outcome of the matter may be a case in your court, I will not stand in the way of your departure.

Go pleasantly, my Chief, and when you again visit us, know that all there is at this kraal is yours.

2

Initiation

My Chief, when last you were with us we were interrupted in our talk by some common folk who saw fit to thrust their trivial affairs upon the notice of their betters at an inconvenient season. It was a matter of trespass which was adjusted by my paying a bag of grain where four had been demanded for the damage done to crops by the trespass of our cattle. It was that avaricious fellow Ntuku, son of Gwabeni. His mouth is as large as a crack in the mud in dry weather, so there should have been no need for him to have opened it so wide in making his demand. He is well called Ntuku the mole. His ways are obscure. It is never known at what unsuitable time and place he may thrust himself up. I will tell you later, my Chief, of a small matter which gave rise to a difference between the people of Gwabeni and those of our clan; but, as I have said, all things must be stated in the order of their happening.

Late one night, after the men had departed to their places, my father sent for me to come to his hut. I went there. The fire was burning low in the centre of the floor. I could just make out in the dusk of the firelight my father's muscular figure. It was for me to wait till he spoke, so for a while there was silence between us. In the flickering light his great form was shadowed on the wall behind him as he sat with his arms resting on his knees and his hands extended towards the fire. At last he drew his blanket round him, spat, rubbed his mouth, then spoke as if addressing the dying embers.

'The man who takes the goat of another and ties it with a riem (a leather thong) is a fool. All riems differ from one another and may be traced to the owner. Grass cords are all alike, and none may say this is the cord of So-and-so.

'When an ox or a horse is to be taken, those of indistinctive colour should be selected, so that they are not readily observed.

'A man who drives the beast of another should drive it with the assurance of an owner, so that the eyes of the inquisitive be not attracted.

'Courteous replies should always be returned to enquiries as to whence you have come, whither you are going and with whose property you are travelling, otherwise suspicion and consequent trouble may arise.

'When questioned, rather than reply directly answer with a question, so that you may receive more information than you give.

'Flattery when applied with discretion is an unction wherewithal to secure the approbation of those in authority.

'When a Chief is met, he should be addressed with respect yet without subservience. It is the custom of Chiefs to be kindly disposed towards those common folk who know how they should comport themselves in the presence of their superiors.'

Between each of these sayings my father paused, so that I was able to commit them speedily to memory and weigh their worth.

When I had undergone the circumcision rites some time before this my father had admonished me as to the duties and responsibilities which would be mine upon entering manhood's estate. Now that I was a grown young man he was giving me further instruction, but of a different kind.

My father was silent for a while, and then, as if for the first time noticing my presence in the hut, he addressed me directly. He instructed me to go to my uncle's kraal, which was some considerable distance from ours, and from my uncle's sheep to take the fattest I could find and bring it home. This order surprised me, but it was not for me to question it, so I at once fetched my sticks and started off. It was a dark night, but I was familiar with the way. I was glad to remember that I was well known to my uncle's dogs, and that I would be able to pacify them should they be inclined to make my presence known. When near the kraal I halted and listened. All was still. I softly whistled in a manner known to dogs. They approached me warily, but at a whispered word they recognised me. I now felt that it was safe for me to get to business. I entered the sheep-fold and quickly selecting a sheep to my liking I caught it by the leg and dragged it out, where I tied it by the neck with my grass rope. I got away from the kraal and took it in a direction opposite to that from which I had approached, making for a place where there was a wide expanse of flat stones and where no spoor would be left; there I turned directly back towards my father's kraal, where I arrived just as dawn was beginning to show. I roused my father, who at once slaughtered the sheep. He instructed me to wrap a heavy stone in the skin and throw it in a deep pool in the river, so that it should not be found. On my return from the river my father told me to dip my hands in the paunch of the sheep and to rub my face with some of the contents. This I did as it was my father's instruction, not knowing what it signified. I learned later that this, together with the taking of the sheep, was an initiation into the secret rites of our clan. If the taking of the sheep were not within a reasonable time laid to my charge, then the initiation would be considered to be complete.

The next day my father instructed me to go to my uncle's

and borrow for him some tobacco. I did not like this, as I was afraid that I might be accused of taking the sheep, and on the way I pondered in my mind as to whether I should not go elsewhere and return saying my uncle had no tobacco. But no, I could not deceive my father, so summoning my courage I went to my uncle's kraal, where I announced the object of my visit. I was asked the news. I said at our place there was no news, but my father was laid up with a chest complaint. I asked after the health of my mother's people and enquired as to their news. My mother's people were all well and there was no news. I was pleased to hear of the good health of my relatives, but I was more pleased to know that the loss of the sheep had not yet been discovered. I should certainly have been told of this had it been known. It was just then that a herdboy came and reported that there was a sheep short in the flock. My uncle, who prized his sheep, was greatly exercised at this information, and at once called out all the men to help trace the spoor. I joined the search party. After a while I came upon my own spoor and thinking quickly I showed it to the men. This they said was the spoor of the thief. I agreed with them. As we proceeded I was complimented upon my ability to follow a spoor over such hard ground. I received this praise with proper modesty. When we came to the place of flat stones all trace was lost, but we were now not far from the kraal of Gwabeni, so it was decided to go straight to that kraal and call upon the people to take up the spoor, which custom required they should do. If they were unable to take the spoor beyond their kraal, then we were entitled to demand from them that the missing sheep be replaced and that we should be compensated for the trouble we had taken in the search. Seek as they would Gwabeni's people found themselves unable to carry on the spoor, so they handed over to us a sheep in the place of the one we had lost and with very bad grace slaughtered an old goat for the refreshment of our search party. The matter of my uncle's lost sheep having been adjusted, and having eaten sufficiently of the tough meat of the goat, we returned to my uncle's kraal. This is the small matter to which I have referred as having brought about discord between Gwabeni's people and our clan.

After obtaining from my uncle a liberal supply of tobacco, I returned home, where I reported to my father the details of what had occurred. He ordered me to have the cattle brought in, and to my great surprise and greater gratification he selected a sleek heifer from the herd and presented it to me.

With this gift there arose between my father and myself a greater understanding than had existed before.

Nkosi, I see that one of your policemen stands without with some kind of a letter in his hand; no doubt it is a message from Mongameli (the Chief Magistrate). These highly placed Chiefs seem to be able to find the moment at which we least desire to be disturbed, but since they are Chiefs it is for us to salute and do our best promptly to carry out their wishes.

3

Of the Manner in which Brandy is Obtained

I received your message, Chief, saying that you would be with us today. Your presence is always welcome. Today I will relate to you the manner in which I obtained brandy for my uncle, who said he was sick; and if your time permits, I will tell you of other matters.

I had learned that there was harmony and friendship between my father and my little father (uncle) from whom I had taken the sheep, so that when I was instructed to go to a neighbouring village to get brandy for my uncle, who said he was sick, I readily undertook the journey. My father had carefully instructed me as to the method of obtaining brandy, which he explained was a somewhat delicate matter. I was to go to the 'Office' (Magistrate's Court), and say that a relative was seriously ill with fever. I was, if questioned, to state in detail the serious symptoms of his ailment, and show that it was necessary to have brandy to mix with certain medicinal herbs of which he knew. I would then, if I had properly carried out these directions, get a paper from the Magistrate which would enable me to get a bottle of brandy at the hotel. I was to induce the man who gave me the brandy to lend me the paper for a while. After I had obtained one bottle I was to hand it to a man named Solani of whom I knew. I was then to return with the paper and obtain a second bottle which was to be delivered to Masimini, a relative of ours. I was to return again and again

15

with the paper and hand the bottles obtained to different people whom my father named and who were known to me as his associates. It was surprising to me how easily I found these people. They just seemed to be there at the moment I wanted them.

It was getting late, so for the last time I returned to the Kanti (canteen) to surrender the Magistrate's paper and with it get my uncle's brandy. I received it, and just as I was going off I was stopped by two policemen. They were Fingoes, a people always ready to pry into affairs which do not concern them. The man who gave me the brandy had evidently noticed them, for he quickly returned to me the paper I had surrendered. I thrust it into my smoking-bag. It was then that these two Fingo policemen barred my way. They took from me my bottle of brandy and said they had arrested me. They took me to a place where there was a white policeman. There was much talk at that place. I was not greatly interested in what was said, but my feelings rebelled at my being kept standing there. So when there was a pause in the conversation I asked for an explanation of all this ceremony at which my presence seemed to be necessary, yet in which I played so very small a part. Six eyes immediately glared upon me, three mouths spoke at once. From these several mouths I understood at last that I had been arrested for having brandy in my possession without having a proper paper. I asked them of what brandy they might be speaking. They thereupon produced the bottle I had obtained at the Kanti. I asked what kind of wizards were they to know that the bottle contained brandy, whereas, as they could well see, it had not been opened, even its little shining hat which stood upon its head had not been removed. There was then silence among them till one of them, finding a means, withdrew the cork and, lifting the bottle high, placing the head in his mouth, allowed a portion of the contents to flow down his interminable throat, whereafter he set the bottle upon a table with the one word 'Brandy'. I was glad to think that I should be able to state to my uncle from the opinion of one who seemed to know about these things that what I was bringing him was really brandy, but what annoyed me was that some of it had been taken by a stranger. Up to this stage I had comported myself with restraint and I hope something of dignity. Here was I, a Xesibe, detained without apparent reason by these gabbling people. I had not yet been permitted to speak, but felt myself as full of words as a sow might be of young ones, so that when there was a suitable pause in the talk I said, 'My Chiefs, if I understand you aright, I have been found with what you say is brandy, not having a proper paper with which to carry the brandy. I have some kind of paper, whether it is such as you require judge for yourselves.' With much ceremony and apparent searching I felt in my smoking-bag. I first took out a box of matches, then a small parcel of roots, then some tobacco and so on, all the contents of my bag. Each article I placed carefully on the table, yet still continued to grope in my bag where all along I had felt the paper they wanted. Then I produced my travelling pass, which I triumphantly handed over. 'Fool,' said the white policeman, 'this is not a permit to have liquor.' He ordered me to be taken to jail. Seeing that this white policeman was becoming impatient and even angry, I took out the paper I had received from the Magistrate and asked if by any chance that was what he required. He opened it out, and after looking at it he chased those Fingoes out of the room where we had been talking, threw the paper at me and told me to 'voetsek' (clear out).

My father had told me to be respectful to my superiors, so saying, 'May all go well with you, my Chief,' I picked up the paper and left. I felt gratified at the thought that the police had not interfered with my business at an earlier stage, otherwise how should I have supplied Solani, Masimini and all the others with that which I had been instructed to secure for them.

Yes, it is wonderful what may be accomplished with one small piece of paper if it is handled with discretion.

4

Of a Troublesome Flock of Sheep

By invitation I spent that night with Solani, who was a distant relative of my father. I left his place at the grey of dawn the following morning. As is known, the road from thereabouts lies for a long distance between two fences with farms on either side. As I came to the place where the farm of Hasha, a white man, lies on both sides of the road, I saw a large flock of sheep crossing the road from one pasturage to another. These sheep seemed to be disturbed by my arrival, for while most of them dashed across quite a number went in front of me along the road between the fences. As I walked on the sheep went on. It was no affair of mine. I continued on my way and the sheep went on in front. It was no affair of mine. So I proceeded till I came to a high ridge where the fences ended and the road continued through open country. The sheep seemed pleased at the change. They went on their way, nibbling at the grass in their progress. To my surprise they took a direction which coincided exactly with my own. I walked on and the sheep went on; they always kept in front of me. I do not wish to repeat my words unnecessarily, but I must again say that this was no affair of mine.

As the sun rose I found myself near the kraal of my uncle Kamteni, whose place is at the foot of the Nsizwa Mountain. Here I turned away from the sheep, which having always been in my way had by the slowness of their progress hindered me in my journey. I went to my uncle's hut and made myself known. My uncle asked for the news from the places I had been visiting. I said there was no news and told him that I had been sent to fetch medicine for my mother's brother, who had said he was sick. He enquired as to the nature of the medicine I had been sent to fetch. When I informed him that it was brandy, he said he had been feeling far from well for the last few days. When I said that my mother's brother was said to be suffering from fever, he told me I had done wisely in obtaining brandy, which was a well-known cure for fever, an ailment with which he himself was frequently afflicted; in fact it was the very sickness which at the moment had laid him prostrate. Our people, he said, were unfortunately subject to the complaint. I produced the bottle of my mother's brother from my smoking-bag; its very appearance seemed to give my uncle relief, and after he had partaken of a dose or two I was satisfied from his improved condition that what the bottle contained was a most efficacious remedy even without the admixture of medicinal roots and herbs.

Kamteni questioned me as to the sheep. I told him how I had come upon the flock and how a portion, to my great inconvenience, had persisted in going in the very direction I was making. He suggested that the sheep seemed now to be quite satisfied to rest, grazing quietly, and they were no longer likely to interfere with my movements.

Since my uncle had put it that way, it was not for me to disagree with him, and as it seemed from the manner of his speech that he desired me to continue on my journey, bidding him a respectful farewell I gathered up my things, including the bottle which still contained a remnant of the medicine.

When my uncle noticed that I had taken up the bottle, he hinted that I would be welcome to spend the day at his kraal and partake of such poor hospitality as it might provide.

Fearing that if I remained I should have nothing to produce to my other uncle save an empty bottle, I excused myself on the plea of having matters of urgency to attend to at home.

I resumed my journey.

5

Of the Charge against Kamteni and the Calling in of a Doctor

As it turned out later it was fortunate for me that the sheep which had accompanied me to Kamteni's remained there, for on a certain day Kayser, a white farmer, came and laid claim to them; he took them away and Kamteni was arrested and put in jail for having stolen them. He engaged a lawyer to talk his case and was for the time being let out on bail. He sent for me and other people of our kraal so that we might talk over the case in order that when it was heard our evidence should agree. I was to state that the sheep belonged to Hasha and not to Kayser the white man who had claimed them, and was to describe how I knew this and how they came to be at Kamteni's kraal. The evidence to be given by each witness was discussed and reviewed so that there should be no disagreement.

In accordance with custom we consulted a doctor, enquiring as to what he might be able to do for us towards the acquittal of Kamteni. This doctor came. He would not speak till we had paid the fee known as Umkhonto (the assegai). We paid this. He said he did not see his way clear to assisting us till we had paid the fee which was necessary to induce him to open his medicine bag. We paid this. He said it was customary for people who consulted him to slaughter a goat. We agreed to do this. Boys were sent to fetch a goat and while the work of slaughtering was proceeding the doctor, whose name by the way was Kwanguba, retired to consider our case.

After a long absence Kwanguba returned. He said ours was a very hard case and that he felt quite exhausted with the work he had so far done in considering it, had we not a little beer wherewith to refresh him. We brought the beer.

By this time the meat of the goat had been cooked. It was apportioned among us and we ate it. When we had finished eating we waited for the advice of Kwanguba as to how we should act at the time of the talking of the case. There was silence, quite a long silence, when one ventured to remind him that having consulted him in this matter we were now prepared to hear his advice. He appeared to be annoyed at this and said we were ignorant people; did we not know that inspiration came when it came, it was a thing which should not be forced and could not be hurried; if we were not satisfied with his methods of handling the case he would withdraw and leave Kamteni to his fate; moreover, he had not yet recovered from his exhaustion.

We were abashed at these remarks and realised that the case was a more difficult one than we had supposed.

Kwanguba returned to his pot of beer and we remained silent.

After the beer was finished he said he was much exercised over the case which, though it might appear easy, was in actual fact one of the most difficult he had ever encountered. There were certain people who hoped for our discomfiture, and before he was able to do anything to our advantage he would have to counteract those influences they had already brought to bear upon the matter. He impressed upon us that the slightest mistake on his part in preparation might end in disaster, as the smallest error on our part in carrying out his instructions would certainly be fatal. He added that, if we did not think that his assistance would bring about the desired result, we were welcome to go elsewhere for aid. We hastened to assure him that we were perfectly satisfied with the work he had done, could do and would do. To prove our confidence in him and our approval of his methods another pot of beer was placed before him. We hoped that this would encourage his endeavours on our behalf and stimulate those unknown forces which brought about inspiration.

It was now getting late and we hoped that Kwanguba would soon express himself. We waited patiently, awed at the prospect of his withdrawing and leaving us unassisted. He continued to take deep draughts from the beer-pot till it was empty, and when he put it aside and called upon one to fill and light a pipe for him, we hoped that the time had arrived when he would tell us things. When we saw the pipe droop from his mouth, his figure loll against the wall and his eyes become staring, we knew that inspiration had come and felt that the issue of our case was safe. After a while he began to sing. We could not quite follow the words of his song, they seemed to run into each other. Knowing that 'the influence' would arise as much from the powers without as from the spirit within him, we were satisfied that there was now a communion between these two forces, and we breathlessly waited for an announcement.

Gradually Kwanguba's voice died down to a mere mumbling, then he became silent, his eyes closed, his body, relaxed and inert, leaned against the hut wall. He was in a trance; he would see things, he would receive revelation!

Silence prevailed, and so we sat for a very long time, fearing that by movement or sound we might rouse him at a moment when inspiration should be upon him.

That matter was settled for us in a surprising fashion. The fire of piled logs which burned in the fireplace in the middle of the hut suddenly collapsed in Kwanguba's direction, scattering a shower of coals upon his bare legs. He sprang up instantly and shook the sparks from his blanket. He cursed us with the names of all our forefathers. He said that we had disturbed him at the very moment when he was about to receive knowledge. When Kamteni had been condemned and sentenced to very many years of imprisonment, the fault would be ours. How could it be expected of a doctor that he should work spells when a crowd of foolish people allowed him to be burnt, and that just at a moment when it was to be revealed to him what he should do for their benefit!

We knew not what to do or say, but one who had more sense than the rest of us ran to the store hut and speedily returned with a large pot of beer, which was placed before Kwanguba, who drank long and deeply.

We felt that by our carelessness we had ruined our cause. We had allowed the fire to fall and burn Kwanguba; we were at fault, and so held our peace, waiting to hear what he might say.

Pushing the now empty beer-pot on one side, Kwanguba delivered himself thus: 'Oh, men of this kraal, you have called me in to assist you in a time of extreme need and I have come to your aid. By your carelessness you have not only damaged your own cause, but you are likely to injure me in the high reputation I bear with the people of these parts; see to it that ye put these matters right and all may still be well. I am now entirely exhausted with the work I have done for you this day; take me to a place where I may rest my weary mind and body.'

We escorted him to a spare hut, where a sleeping mat was spread for him with a pot of beer placed beside it. Wishing him a peaceful and restful night, we withdrew.

We rejoined the others who had remained in the hut in which we had been. None dared break the silence. Several sat with the palms of their hands over their mouths, which

25

indicated that they were seriously at a loss.

Kamteni it was who spoke first, and it was right that this should have been so; he, being head of the kraal, was responsible for anything that might happen within its precincts. The burning of the doctor and all that meant was a matter with which he would have to deal.

'Men,' said he, 'we are faced with a very serious situation and it behoves us to act promptly and suitably. I have considered the matter and I have concluded that we have been careless on an occasion when extreme discretion was required of us. Let us very early in the morning drive a fat goat to the hut occupied by Kwanguba and offer to slaughter it for him; there is just a remote chance that he may refuse it; in any case the gift, if coupled with a pot of beer, may please him. I know that he will later expect me to present him with a heifer as propitiation for the evil he says we have done him. I am prepared to produce this heifer if occasion arises. What say ye?'

We all agreed that he had spoken well and as a large-minded man would, whereat he seemed pleased, so much so that he ordered an underling to place before us a large pot of beer.

Early next morning, as arranged, we took a goat and a pot of beer to Kwanguba. These he accepted with good grace, which led us to hope that he would now advise us in the matter of the case, but this was not to be.

Speaking more in sorrow than in anger, he said it might quite easily have been a dead body rather than a live person we were now regarding. The result of our causing him to be burnt and suddenly wakened from his trance might have been fatal. Did we not know this? He was fortunate in escaping with his life; as it was the shock had made him ill and he would be able to do no work that day.

We were greatly disappointed at this news but, after

all, things were not so bad as they might have been. Had Kwanguba died at the kraal as the result of things for which we were responsible, what evil might not have befallen us?

He remained at the kraal for five days, during which time he held aloof from us.

We were pleased when at last he came into a hut where we were sitting with beer.

After the pot had been handed to him and he had partaken he spoke: 'Oh, men of this kraal, in these days of my seclusion much has been revealed to me.

'As different medicines are required for the treatment of different ailments, so different medicines must be provided for each of the matters connected with this case. The Magistrate will have to be doctored, so that he may take a favourable view; Kamteni will have to be doctored as a protection from the evil spells of others; and the witnesses will require medicine so that their tongues may not cause them to be entrapped in their evidence.'

We agreed that all these doctorings were necessary.

Kwanguba said that the difficulties of the case had almost overcome him, but he now felt he would in due course be justified in demanding from us umlandu – the fee which would be payable on Kamteni's acquittal. He would come the day before the case and provide all that was necessary; he would even go with us to the Court so as to ensure the proper working of his medicines.

With this he left.

It is good of you, Chief, to spare so much of your time listening to the gabbling of an old man. I am now weary with talking, but if you will honour us with your presence on another day I will tell you more.

6

Of Matters Concerning
Kamteni's Case

Bayete, Nkosi! Let us go and sit in the sunshine beside the cattle kraal and I will continue my story from where I broke off when weariness overtook me.

On a certain day a policeman came to our kraal asking for me. He said he had brought a paper from the Magistrate commanding me to appear before the Court to give evidence in the case of Kamteni.

I said I did not know that paper, nor did I require it, as I being the one who knew all about Kamteni's case intended to appear before the Court and testify to what I knew. It was right that the Magistrate should wish to see me, as I was the very one who could tell him all about Kamteni's case; but as to the paper, that could be taken back to the Magistrate and used for bringing some unwilling witness before the Court. As for me I was going to the Court.

The policeman got off his horse and thrust the paper at me in a very insolent manner. I looked to see where my stick was, but the matter ended there, as the policeman rode off leaving the paper with me. I wished then that Kwanguba had supplied me with my medicine. I should have tested its efficacy by doing something bad to that policeman with it.

I understood that I should be paid money for attending Court, and on the strength of this I borrowed a pound from a friend with which I bought a pair of trousers and a pair of boots at the Venkile (store) of a white man named Madevu. I did not like these articles of dress, but I felt that it might, in a measure, assist Kamteni if I appeared in the presence of the Magistrate clad in the clothing of the white people. It would be a mark of respect to the Court, which I felt sure would not be overlooked.

The boots caused me a great deal of discomfort when I put them on, no less the trousers; but I was prepared to suffer something if it might help towards the acquittal of my uncle Kamteni.

I tried on my boots and trousers from time to time and walked about in them. They were greatly admired by my friends, and for that reason I began to have some kind of liking for them, feeling sure that the Magistrate would notice them and be favourably influenced.

Kwanguba came on the day before the case to Kamteni's kraal, where those of us concerned had assembled. He and Kamteni spent a long time together in a hut, and when my uncle reappeared his face wore an expression of satisfaction. I never heard the details of his doctoring, but I learned that he had been given a small parcel of very strong roots; these he was to keep concealed under his blanket, and while he was in Court he was to hold them in his hand, keeping his eyes steadily fixed on the face of the Magistrate.

I was at first disappointed in my medicine, the parcel was so small; but when Kwanguba told me I would have to keep the medicine in my mouth while giving my evidence I was satisfied. He said this was a special medicine for tongues; it would make my tongue so slippery that it would glide through and overcome difficult questions with ease, at the same time it would make my speech smooth and pleasing.

This seemed to me to be a very good medicine and I decided to try it at once. It looked like a little piece of dry stick.

I placed it in my mouth so that it lay between my lower teeth and my cheek. Saliva began to flow. I knew that this was the fat that was to make my tongue slippery and yet sweet.

I went back to the men and joined in the conversation. The medicine worked. I felt that I spoke in a clever manner with a pleasant voice.

After a while I withdrew and removed my medicine from my mouth. Carefully wrapping it up, I placed it in my smoking-bag. It would not do to use it too much before it was actually needed, it might lose its strength.

On the day of the case we were very early astir preparing for the journey to the Court. It was the first time for me to experience a thing of this kind, but I had no misgivings. Had not I been instructed as to the manner in which I should comport myself in the presence of Great Ones, and would not I be dressed suitably to make a good appearance? Above all, I had upon me medicine of which people knew not.

So that my new clothing should not be disfigured by the dust of travel, I tied my trousers around my neck and hung my boots on a stick which I carried over my shoulder.

I felt that when I appeared before the Magistrate I would surely create a good impression, when I would be a credit to my people and probably be the means of saving my uncle from a long term of imprisonment.

My heart swelled within me as in anticipation I thought with pride and pleasure over these matters.

I should that day by my words and acts establish for myself a reputation. I imagined that at a later stage people might whisper as I passed them: 'Look, that man you see there, the one who carries himself so well; he is Ntsukumbini, he it was who spoke so cleverly in the case of Kamteni that even the Magistrate was overcome with admiration.'

I felt that a Court was a good thing, a place where people

of ability might distinguish themselves. In my breast arose pleasant feelings towards the Magistrate. I could almost see the kindly and gracious manner in which he would regard me, Ntsukumbini, when I stood before him and delivered my testimony. As for those Fingo policemen who had behaved so rudely towards me in the matter of brandy, if I saw them I should spit in a manner which would clearly show them that they were not the lords of the earth they seemed to consider themselves. If the Magistrate should happen to observe the manner in which I spurned them, so much the better.

I felt how anxious the Magistrate must be to hear my statement, which would once and for all clear up all doubt and make everything plain.

These and many other things passed through my mind as we journeyed to the Court. The evil thought for an instant came to me: what if I kept the Magistrate waiting for a few moments? Would that not enhance the importance of my entrance to the Court when I did appear? I rejected this thought directly it had been born. I would that day attain sufficient distinction without resorting to methods which might savour of discourtesy.

Yes, it was a good day, it was *my* day, the whole world was good and all people were my friends.

I have not referred to those in whose company I was travelling. It seemed to me not to be a time for thinking of people who were that day to be less privileged than I.

Almost before I realised it we were upon the outskirts of the village, and here was I still carrying my boots and trousers which I had entirely forgotten while pondering over important affairs. I asked the other people to halt a while to permit of my clothing myself.

It seemed to me my boots had grown smaller while I carried them and that my trousers had been bewitched in such a manner as to cause me difficulty in fastening that row of buttons which is the means of closing up this kind of garment in the front. It may have been that the bread made of green mealies which we had eaten on the way had had a slight swelling effect, for it was the upper buttons which gave me the greatest anxiety and trouble, so much so that at one stage of my dressing I suggested to those who were assisting me that the trousers be put on the opposite way to that in which they were usually worn and that the buttons be left loose; as I should not at any stage be turning my back upon the Magistrate he would be unlikely to observe that the buttons had not been fastened. Those who were used to the wearing of trousers said that it would be unseemly for me to put on the clothing of white people except in the way it was customary for it to be worn. The white people were always ready to take offence where none was intended, and might look upon this as a deliberate disregard of their customs.

I managed at last with the assistance of my companions to clothe myself, but I liked this dress of the white people less than before.

We eventually reached the Court House, where we found quite a number of people assembled. I noticed with surprise that the conversation was not in regard to our case, but about ordinary trivial matters. What astounded me was the people didn't even seem to know about our case; how was such a thing possible?

I heard one man ask Kamteni what business had brought us to the Court. He said it was a small matter concerning sheep in which a mistake had been made. I admired Kamteni for his reticence, but I marvelled at the other man's ignorance.

The time for the hearing of cases was approaching. I found that matters other than ours were to be heard, trivial things no doubt which the Magistrate would dispose of in a few minutes so as to be able to settle down to the important business of the day.

We waited and waited, but there was no mention of our case. Meantime the sun was getting hot and my boots began to bite. I endured this for a while, then went off to a secluded spot where I took off my boots and loosened a few of the buttons of my trousers.

I had hardly done this when I heard my name called in a loud voice. I responded with dignity. When I saw it was one of the Fingo policemen I took no great notice of him, but began to work with my boots, which were now refusing to go on to my feet.

The policeman spoke to me in a rude manner, saying I was to come at once, as the Court was waiting for my evidence.

I had not succeeded in putting on my boots, so I followed the policeman, carrying them. I entered the Court Room and was then hustled along in a rough manner till I found myself in the very front, where I was instructed to enter a sort of little square box.

I carefully put down my boots, then boldly turning to the Magistrate I raised my hand and in a loud voice so that all might hear I saluted him in true Xesibe fashion: 'Bayete, Nkosi, Dumezweni!'

I had rehearsed this scene in my mind many times. I had heard that the Magistrate liked his name of 'Dumezweni' (renowned throughout the world) and I was sure that he would be glad to hear that I knew it.

To my surprise I was told to be quiet. Then I realised what was wrong; having been taken by surprise by the policeman, I had forgotten my medicine. I instantly slipped it into my mouth, but before I was quite ready I was asked to explain why I had kept the Court waiting. So as to gather my senses I replied: 'I? Are you addressing me?' The interpreter, an un-

33

couth fellow, said of course he was addressing me: who else would it be?

By this time my senses had gathered and to my great comfort I felt the medicine beginning to work. Blessing Kwanguba in my mind for what he had done for me, I said: 'My Chief, I am asked why I have kept the Court waiting.' Words, and sweet words, were ready to fall from me as honey drips from a bruised honeycomb. 'It was like this: I borrowed a pound from a friend of mine whose name is Nyaniso, son of K'mbela. This man lives at a little distance from us, a valley separating our homesteads. With the pound I borrowed from Nyaniso I went to the store of Madevu, a white man with whom our people have always done business. From Madevu I bought a pair of trousers and a pair of boots. For the trousers I paid seven shillings and threepence, for the boots I paid ten shillings and two shillings and a sixpence and threepence, so was the pound I borrowed from Nyaniso spent.'

Here the Magistrate, through the interpreter, asked what in the whole earth I was talking about.

As my medicine was working very nicely, I was able to answer promptly: 'My lord, I am explaining how it came that I did not appear before you the instant your messenger came announcing your wish to see me.' I picked up my boots and holding them up before the Magistrate I continued: 'My lord, if I have erred, these two people are the ones who have caused me to be at fault. At Madevu's shop where I bought them there were at that time not many boots and I had to be content with these, though somewhat small. I find now that these are the boots of one foot and this had inclined me to walk sideways like a crab. These boots bit me, so that I had to take them off and that at a time when this case which I am about to explain to you was to be called.'

I had a lot more to say, but I was here interrupted by the

interpreter, who at a sign from the Magistrate gabbled off a lot of words in my own language. He said them so quickly that I was unable to catch their import, so I said: 'I? Are you addressing me?'

The interpreter looked at me sternly and said, 'Hold up two fingers of your right hand and say, "So help me, God".'

Now I required no help from anyone, being fortified with good medicine; moreover, I did not know which two fingers it was required I should hold up; so to comply fully with what appeared to be the custom of the Court I held up my right hand with all its fingers and repeated what the interpreter had told me to say. If that was the manner in which the Magistrate desired to be saluted, I was satisfied to salute him in that way.

It appeared that the business upon which I had come was now about to begin.

7

The Hearing of Kamteni's Case

As I have mentioned before, I was not familiar with the manner in which cases are conducted in the Court of a Magistrate. The way in which this case began surprised me. I had gone there to tell the Magistrate what I knew, having been called there for that purpose, whereas a white policeman stood up and began to tell *me* things. He told me I lived in Gamtweni's Location, and that I was a native peasant, then he went on to tell me all about the sheep that had gone to Kamteni's.

All this time I assented politely with 'Ewe Nkosi' (Yes, Chief) to what this white policeman said. This was to encourage him to continue his story and to show him that I was interested.

Then he began to tell me things that astonished me, things that had never happened, but it was his story, and it was not for me to rudely disagree with him, so I continued to assent with 'Ewe Nkosi'.

At this stage a little man with a bald head and a red face jumped up out of his seat and spoke with heat to the white policeman. I did not like this, as the policeman was telling me things of interest. Yet I was anxious for the time when I could be called upon to speak, as I felt my medicine was working nicely. I wondered what the little bald-headed man had to do with the case.

The white policeman continued his story. He said Kamteni had kept the sheep, they had been found in his possession; he knew they were Kayser's, and therefore he had stolen them. To all these statements I assented with 'Ewe Nkosi'. When I should be called upon to state the truth of the matter, the Court would hear a very different story.

When the white policeman had finished speaking to me he sat down. Little bald head got up and spoke to the Magistrate, who turned to me. He said: 'You have told the Court that Kamteni stole these sheep and you have described the manner in which he stole them.' I was surprised that the Magistrate should put words into my mouth, so I said: 'My lord, I have not yet spoken; I have said nothing about Kamteni or the sheep.'

Then the face of the Magistrate got red. He said the prosecutor had questioned me, and that I had answered 'Yes' to all his questions, thereby agreeing with all he said.

I asked what questions were these; the man whom he called the prosecutor had been telling me a lot of things, but had asked nothing.

I explained that it was not our custom to disagree with a teller of tales in the midst of his story. It was our custom to show by assenting that we were following what he said and that we were interested.

At this little bald head seemed much pleased, and I concluded that somehow my medicine was doctoring him. He got up and asked me to tell what I knew, so I went on with the true story, and when I showed that the sheep belonged to Hasha and not to Kayser he smiled in such a way that I knew he was very much impressed with what I had said, though I did not know then what he had to do with the case.

Then there was a lot of talk between bald head and the man they called the prosecutor, that is the white policeman who had spoken to me. After their talk the Magistrate said: 'Kamteni is accused of stealing Kayser's sheep. The sheep are not Kayser's, but Hasha's, so Kamteni is acquitted.'

Kamteni sprang up and in a loud voice saluted the Magistrate: 'Bayete Nkosi!' and then we all went out.

Kwowu! that medicine of Kwanguba! Kamteni paid a fat cow and calf for it later on. We all considered these had been well earned by our doctor.

Little bald head was afterwards paid a lot of money for talking the case (I learned then that he was Kamteni's lawyer), but after all it was the medicine which secured Kamteni's acquittal.

8

Concerning Doctors

When the result of the case became known to the people in our parts, the reputation of Kwanguba was firmly established.

We know that the white people regard the powers of our doctors lightly, but was not Kamteni's case a proof of their ability? I am able to say now with safety, as the thing is long past, that Kamteni did take those sheep and as I have told I helped in the taking, but merely because they were taken from Hasha and not from Kayser Kamteni was acquitted! I cannot think that the laws of the white people are all foolishness, and I could not suggest that the Magistrate Dumezweni was an ignorant person; I can only conclude that Kwanguba's medicine acted in such a way as to lead the white people away from a decision which seemed to be the only reasonable one to a point of view entirely in Kamteni's favour. In the Courts of our Chiefs a thief never escapes.

As is known, we have doctors of several kinds; there is the Xwele, who from medicines made of roots and herbs cures people of their bodily ailments; there is the Gqira who, added to a skill in medicines, has a knowledge of supernatural agencies; there is the Gqwira, who is a diviner, also a finder of witches and wizards; and there is the doctor, who makes rain, having some control over the powers of the skies.

It may be that any of these has skill extending beyond the powers usually attributed to him, that is to say the Xwele may know something of rain-making while not professing to be an expert in that matter, as a Gqwira might have a knowledge of medicinal herbs without laying a special claim to the ability to cure people of sickness with medicine.

In the same way, again, our people know certain medicines of which the white doctors have no knowledge.

When a beast dies of anthrax we are able to eat the meat with immunity, either placing herbs with it when it is cooked or drinking a medicine prepared from herbs before we eat. The white people say the carcass should be buried deep, so that no person or animal shall be infected with the disease.

Was there not the case of our own headman who having unwittingly eaten of anthrax meat became sick? He sent his own messenger to the Magistrate to report his illness. Is it not known that the messenger was sent to the white doctor who, when he heard that the headman had eaten of anthrax meat and was ill as a consequence, said: 'I can do nothing; go to your own doctors'? Is it not known that the headman was cured by our own people and that he lived for many years thereafter?

And yet the white people regard our doctors lightly.

I must say this, that it is not now with our doctors as it was in earlier days. The Xwele, having been instructed by his father who was also a Xwele, as was his father before him, was a Xwele and nothing else. So it was with the Gqwira and the rain-maker. Knowledge was handed down from father to son and from father to son and from father to son. The mystic secrets of each were closely guarded. When it came to the time for the son to succeed to the knowledge of the parent, the son passed through a time of initiation: he fasted over long periods, he purified himself, he danced and danced and still danced so that his body was like to fall asunder, he held aloof from the people so that the secret inspiration might come upon him, and so in the end having undergone many privations as

40

well as other bodily and mental tests he was justified in coming forth asserting that he had 'twasaed', that he was renewed in body and mind and that he was fit and ready to carry on the profession of his ancestors.

In these days we find new doctors arising. Whence they obtained their knowledge we know not. It seems they are a lesser people than those whom we knew. Even a Xwele, who is the lowest of the order, will not admit himself at fault if he should happen to be consulted in regard to the matter of rain-making. Rather than refer the enquiries to a man who does know about such things, the Xwele will apply his immature knowledge to the matter and demand a fee for a thing he is unable to bring about.

As I have said, the white people have little trust in the knowledge of our doctors. Let me just mention the case of Madubela, a matter by which the reputation of Kwanguba was once and for all established with us.

Shortly after the case of Kamteni, Madubela, who was himself a doctor, endeavoured to belittle the achievements of Kwanguba. These two happened to meet at a place where there was beer.

Madubela had been consulted in regard to certain money which had been buried by a person, since deceased; but he could not find it. He had also been consulted in regard to the cause of the death of certain children, and hesitated to indicate the person responsible.

It was at this stage that Kwanguba appeared in the neighbourhood, fresh from his success in the case of Kamteni, and it was at this time that he and Madubela met at the place I have spoken of where there was beer.

Madubela stated to those who were intimate with him that it was the lawyer who had secured Kamteni's acquittal and that it was not because of Kwanguba's medicines. This thing and others mentioned by Madubela to the disparagement of Kwanguba became known.

These statements were of course passed on to Kwanguba, who for a long time remained silent. Madubela, thinking that Kwanguba's silence was prompted by fear, persisted in remarks of a nature calculated to do damage.

At last Kwanguba arose, saying: 'Where is this little fellow who questions my powers? If he persists in his foolishness, a bad thing will happen to him.'

Madubela stood up and said: 'I am the little fellow who says that Kamteni was acquitted by lawyers' wiles, while you, Kwanguba, claimed all the credit and received payment.'

Kwanguba drew himself up to his full height and, staring for a moment at Madubela, said: 'Is it you, little thing, who questions my powers? You have been an annoyance to me and must be removed. Today I will cause the lightning to strike you, so prepare for your end.' So saying, Kwanguba went away without a further word.

A big thunderstorm had been brewing and the people who had assembled at that kraal began to leave for their homes, among them Madubela, who had made no answer to Kwanguba's threat.

Soon the storm broke, lightning flashed and thunder rumbled, rain fell in torrents. The people hastened through the pouring rain. When Madubela and those with him reached a high eminence known as Nqutu there was a flash with an instant crash. The people there all fell to the earth stunned; the one who never rose again was Madubela.

The facts of this matter are well known and can be vouched for by many who saw the dead body of Madubela.

And yet the white people regard the powers of our doctors lightly.

9

Of the Method of Witch-finding

I have told of the death of Madubela, which was caused by the agency of Kwanguba.

I do not wish to finish with the matter of doctors before I tell of a thing that made the fame of Kwanguba still greater.

I have made mention of Gwabeni and his son Ntuku the mole. Now Gwabeni was sick, he had been sick for a long time. He had drunk much medicine, but got no better. He called in Kwanguba to ascertain from him who was depriving the medicines of their curing properties. Kwanguba went to the kraal and the people of our place went with him. It is customary in such cases for the people round about to gather at the kraal concerned, so that when we arrived at Gwabeni's there was a considerable assemblage of people. We all entered a hut where places were found for us. Beer was provided and passed round. Ntuku on behalf of his father stated the case to the people. He expected that Kwanguba would speak. Kwanguba remained silent. Ntuku continued to speak, repeating the facts of the matter. Kwanguba remained silent. Ntuku ceased from speaking and sat down. The people waited for something to be said by one whose place it might be to speak, but no one rose up. The beer-pot circulated, was replenished and was again passed round. Kwanguba retired from the hut. Men drank beer in silence.

After a while Kwanguba returned and sat down in his

43

place. People knew that he was full of words and waited for his speech.

At last he rose up and said: 'Men of this place. I have been called here regarding a certain matter of which you know. Sickness has visited this kraal and refuses to be removed. I know who has caused this sickness, and I know by what means it has been brought here. Notwithstanding my knowledge I am here and now withdrawing from the matter, and will from now on have no further dealings with it. Seek ye advice and remedy elsewhere.' So saying, Kwanguba gathered up his belongings and left the kraal.

The people were astounded. Never before was a case known where a doctor professed knowledge, and yet was not prepared to disclose it.

It was very long afterwards that the facts of this matter became known to us. We learned that Gwabeni had secretly given it out that my mother by evil influences had caused his illness. This becoming known to Kwanguba, he being our friend refused to act in the matter in spite of liberal offers on the part of Gwabeni for whom there was nothing else to do than call in another doctor. This man responded readily to the call, and as before we all assembled at the kraal.

Ntuku stated the facts upon which the doctor had been called in. The new doctor thereupon began to dance. He danced till the sweat rolled off him in great beads, his eyeballs rolled in their sockets, each muscle in his body he would cause in turn to quiver.

Then he said: 'I have been called in regard to a matter of sickness.'

We agreed to that and clapped our hands. We continued to clap our hands as the doctor proceeded: 'I have been called in about the sickness of an elderly man.'

Gwabeni's people agreed to this more loudly and clapped

their hands in a manner that indicated their approval.

The doctor continued: 'This sickness has fallen upon an elderly man who is head of this kraal.'

Gwabeni's people assented loudly to this and continued to clap their hands.

The doctor proceeded: 'This sickness has been caused by a certain man.'

Gwabeni's people assented in a very feeble manner to that, and though the clapping of hands proceeded the doctor knew by the feebleness of the assent that he had made a mistake.

He proceeded: 'The head of this kraal has been caused to be sick by the agency of a woman.'

Gwabeni's people agreed loudly.

'The head of this kraal has been made sick by a woman who has had children.'

Gwabeni's people assented loudly.

'The head of this kraal has been made sick by a woman who is beyond the age of child-bearing.'

Gwabeni's people agreed more loudly.

So the doctor felt his way. When he went on to say something which brought him nearer towards indicating my mother as the cause of the illness, so Gwabeni's people assented the more loudly, till at last there could be no mistake as to who was the supposed witch – it was our mother. We of our kraal hastily withdrew, made with all speed for our home and there waited watchfully for the thing that would befall us. We waited and watched, and as nothing happened, towards the early hours of morning one after another fell asleep. We were suddenly awakened by a voice shouting, 'We are being burnt.' We rushed out to find that my mother's hut had been set on fire. One pulled out the flaming thatch while another by some means got on the roof and poured water on the flames, so that the hut was saved.

Now in most cases where a thing of this kind happens at a kraal the people of that kraal would remove to a place far distant, but my mother refused to move, protesting that, as we well knew, she was no witch and had never wilfully brought evil upon any man, woman or child. We knew that she spoke truly. I would say this of my own mother as a matter of course, but all our neighbours knew that my mother was a person full of kindness and kindly acts.

We determined that we would stay. We did stay and there the matter ended.

Look kindly, Chief, upon the feebleness of an old man and permit me now to withdraw. We will meet and talk on other days.

10

Concerning Three Fat Cows

It is a long time, my Chief, since you visited this place, but your present of tobacco reassures me and makes me know that you have not been offended with me; so I will without delay go on with my story, since you never seem to tire hearing of my foolish doings.

Late one night Kamteni arrived at our kraal. He roused my father and together they went out into the darkness. On their return my father told me to go to a certain spot, which he described, where he said I would see something. I went there and saw three fine fat cows. I returned and reported what I had seen.

My father instructed me to take the cows to the kraal of Bangeni, a relative of ours who lived two days' journey from us. I asked where was the pass for the cows. My father looked at me with displeasure, and said: 'What is this talk of passes? Do as you are told. Take the cows to Bangeni, and wait at his kraal four days, after which Bangeni will give you something to bring back to me.'

Now it is contrary to law to drive stock without a pass, and I knew of cases where people had been detained because they had no pass for the stock they were driving; so I looked about among my belongings and found an old pass, on this I wrote down as well as I was able the description of the three cows and also added other information which it was necessary the pass should show. I was glad then that I had learned to write, but still my writing did not look nice – not so nice as the other writing on the pass.

I took the cows and started off. It was now about midnight. I carefully avoided all kraals, so that I should not be bothered with questions from inquisitive people. As dawn broke I found myself in the neighbourhood of Emqokweni River, which, as is known, flows through very rugged country. As the sun rose I placed the cows in a secluded spot near the river, where the grass was good. I myself went to the top of a neighbouring hill and took up a position where I could both observe the cows and watch the surrounding country, while keeping out of sight.

As the day grew I saw people of the kraals in the neighbourhood going about their business: the women went to the fields to hoe while the men came out to sit in the sun beside their cattle-folds, to smoke and talk; the lads attended to the calves. The young men put the cattle out to graze. All these things I saw at a great distance. The people looked like so many ants.

Having travelled all night I was tired and very sleepy. I could feel my head becoming heavy and full of sleep, yet I knew I must keep awake. Suddenly I became aware of a thing that made me wide awake. A young man was driving a herd of cattle in a direction which it seemed would bring him to the very spot in which my three cows were grazing. This must be prevented. I gathered up my things and made my way down the hill. I was fortunate in coming upon a well-trodden path. Had this not been so, I might have been questioned as to why I walked aimlessly across the veld whereas there were well-known paths leading from one place to another.

After a while I came up to the young man who was driving the herd of cattle. I greeted him with 'Good day, child of our people.' He replied with cordiality and asked whence I had come and whither I was going. I said I had come from the Xesibe country and was proceeding on the instruction of my father to a place eastward in regard to a matter of the payment of dowry for the daughter of my father's brother. This young man was much younger than I, and it pleased him to think that one so much his senior should be ready to discuss with him intimate family affairs of importance.

After a pleasant interchange of news the young man suggested that I should visit the kraal of his people, of which he said Dukiswa was the head. I agreed to go with him, but asked how he would be able to escort me to Dukiswa's, seeing the lands were full of young crops and on that account he would not be able to leave his cattle. He said that if I would not mind walking slowly he would drive his herd towards Dukiswa's while the animals grazed on the way.

This was what I wanted – to draw him away from the place where I had left my three cows.

I had learned from this young man something of his family affairs, so it was easy for me to enter the kraal with a salutation appropriate and pleasing, greeting Dukiswa with his isibongo (phrase or song of salutation). He desired to know from me how I was aware of his isibongo. I replied that there was no one in the countryside who did not know the isibongo of so important a person as Dukiswa. I was remembering that my father had said flattery was a pleasing unction, and I proceeded to apply it, with the result that a goat was slaughtered for me, we having found in the course of conversation that I was distantly related to the people of the kraal.

All this while I had been thinking of certain three cows grazing in a secluded glade. I did not wish to break rudely away from the hospitality that had been shown me, but as the afternoon wore on I felt that I must be about my father's business. I would have to go back some little distance on the path by which I had come in order to pick up the three cows. How was I to do this without attracting attention to my movements?

I thought of a plan. I felt in my smoking-bag. 'Tyo!' said I, 'my silanda (an implement for extracting thorns) is missing. I must have left it at the place at which I last halted for a rest, where I was using it to extract a thorn from my foot.' The people in the kindness of their hearts offered to give me a silanda. I said the one I had lost had been presented to me by an uncle who had always been well disposed towards me and from whom I expected other and more valuable gifts. If at any time I appeared before him without the thing he had given me, unpleasantness might result.

The young man whom I had first met offered to accompany me to the place where I had last halted to help search for the silanda. I made it plain that his kraal had already overwhelmed me with kindness, and that, even though our people might be distantly related, I could not expect them to add anything to what they had already done for me.

Asking them to excuse me and thanking them for their hospitality, I withdrew and went on my way. I returned along the path by which I had come, and when I arrived at the place where I had rested on the top of the hill I looked round about. No one from the kraals below appeared to be noticing my movements. I saw the three cows grazing not far from the spot where I had left them. Waiting till dusk fell, I went down and, picking up the cows, proceeded on my journey.

I travelled throughout the night. As dawn broke and just as I was topping a rise, I came face to face with a policeman. It seemed to me to be an unusual time for the police to be about, but after observing this one for a moment it was clear to me that he had been combining pleasure with duty, and that whatever work he might have been engaged upon he had found time to spend the night at an umjadus (a beer drink and dance). He was very full of beer. He swayed in his saddle as he said to me, in a thick voice: 'Halt, fellow! Whither away with those cattle?'

Observing his condition I answered with boldness: 'Policeman, I am no fellow of yours. I am proceeding on the business of respectable people.'

He said: 'A person who drives cattle at this time of night is a thief. By what authority do you move about in the night with cattle?'

I said: 'Authority like what?'

He said: 'You know quite well what I mean. Where is your pass?'

I said: 'Policeman, if you stay talking with people by the roadside you are wasting the time of Government, and I will tell your master Dumezweni about it.'

He was angered at this and made at me with his sjambok, but he was so unsteady in his saddle that it was easy to avoid him. 'Your pass, fellow; where is your pass?' he shouted.

I took out the pass which, as I have already said, I had prepared for just such an occasion.

The policeman looked at the pass for a long time; then, gazing at me, said: 'On this pass is the writing of two people; what kind of a pass is this?'

I replied: 'I am not responsible for the writing of passes. The writing on my pass appears to me to be good, in that it permits me to go about my business in a proper way. I have heard it said that people who have drunk much beer sometimes see two things where there is only one. It may be thus with you, as you say there are two writings. If you, as a servant of the Government, have time to gossip with every man you meet by the roadside about writing, merely to show that you have passed Standard Three, there is something wrong with you, or the Government. Put your name on my pass, and let me go, lest I bring the matter to the notice of Dumezweni, who will deal with you.'

I had delivered this speech with indignation, and the policeman seemed to be confused by it. He searched through his pockets and produced a very short piece of pencil. After sucking at this like a hungry calf he wrote his name on my pass and went on his way.

I continued my journey, and very late that night I was able to hand over the cows to Bangeni.

11

Concerning Three Fine Horses

In the morning I enquired for Bangeni and was told that he had gone on a journey. I noticed that the three cows I had brought were no longer in the kraal and I realised that they had also gone on a journey.

As instructed by my father, I waited the four days at the kraal, and late in the evening of the fourth day Bangeni returned. He told me to go to a certain place where he said I would see something. I went there and saw three fine horses. They were of a dark bay colour, rather short and thickset. I reported to Bangeni what I had seen. He said: 'Take these horses to your father; it will not be asked by him whence you have obtained them. As you proceed on your journey, on no account must you omit at the Mtwaku Stream to observe the custom. There you will see a cairn of stones. Pick up a stone and place it on the cairn, asking it to give you good fortune.'

I bade farewell to Bangeni and went off with the horses. I now realised I was taking part in the business of my father and of my uncles. This gave me a proud feeling. I remembered the advice my father had given me long ago and resolved to follow it carefully.

It was a very misty night and it was unlikely that I would be observed as I travelled along. I rode one of the horses and led the other two.

I rode on for a long time in the dark till I came to near

the Mtwaku Stream. I dismounted and looked for the cairn, which I found beside the path. I picked up a stone and placed it on the cairn with the words, 'Amandla sivivane' (Give me strength, oh cairn). I mounted and went on my way. I was sure the cairn would give me strength and good fortune on my journey. I felt so emboldened that I decided not to leave the horses during the day in a secluded spot as I had done with the cows. I would ride on with the air of a possessor. I got on to the main road. I passed several people who, apart from giving the ordinary salutation, took little notice of me.

Late in the day I met Ntuku, son of Gwabeni, of whom I have made mention. This Ntuku was of common stock, as are all his people. He being a neighbour of ours, custom demanded that we should pass the time of day with each other. What surprised me was that he made no serious enquiry about the horses. He merely remarked upon their good appearance without enquiring as to whence they came. With us such a thing is unusual. It is always desired to know whence 'things' come and for what purpose they are being taken from one place to another.

No questions of this nature being asked me by Ntuku, I became suspicious.

We parted, he went his way and I went mine, but as soon as he was out of sight I tied two of the horses to a tree and rode with the third as fast as I could round behind a neighbouring hillock and up to near its top, where I dismounted. I went on foot to the top of the little hill to see what I might see.

Away in the distance I saw Ntuku making his way by a circuitous route as fast as his horse could put its feet to the ground for a kraal which lay right upon the way I would take. This was enough to show me that he was, as I had always supposed, a treacherous fellow.

But it was not for a common fellow like this to put fear

into me. I came down from out the little hill and proceeded with my three horses along the main road, feeling ready for anything that might befall me. If the wit of a common fellow such as Ntuku, born of common people, was to be better than mine, so let it be. I had observed the custom at the cairn and trusted that all would be well.

As I proceeded on my way three men suddenly appeared from round a bend in the road, coming from the direction of the huts to which I had seen Ntuku go.

They greeted me pleasantly enough, but then began to enquire of me as to the horses in a less friendly manner, showing it was their intent to find me at fault. Little as I knew of the horses, I found answers to all their questionings such as should satisfy any reasonable man. These men were older than I and of wider experience, but I had knowledge of certain things they knew not of. Kwanguba had supplied me with medicines for which I had paid dearly. Some of these medicines were to be taken by myself at any time of difficulty or danger to secure success and safety, others had to be used upon those who desired my discomfiture. One of these was an Mhlabelo – of which there are many different kinds – a round root rather smaller than my closed fist. If this root were applied in a proper manner to a broken limb, it caused the broken bones to join up speedily. If it were taken internally, it caused a person to fall asleep immediately. We had used this kind of Mhlabelo for catching baboons. We soaked grain in the juice and placed it in places frequented by baboons. After eating the grain, at first they became very drunk, then they lay down and went to sleep, when we would go up and kill them.

But, my Chief, I am not telling you of medicines. I am telling the manner in which I carried out my father's instructions in regard to the things he said I should receive from Bangeni.

The men went on with their questioning. At last one said:

'These horses are stolen and you are our thief.'

They ordered me to go with them to their kraal. They took the horses and put them in the cattle-fold. Me they took into a hut. I made it appear as if I were very down-hearted and that I was submitting quietly to the arrest. After a while they went out of the hut, fastening the door upon me. I took some of Kwanguba's medicine and chewed it. This made me feel hopeful. While I was deeply thinking as to how I should next act, my eyes rested upon a small empty beer-pot. This pot would be used for drinking beer; it would be used by my captors. I must doctor it. I quickly got out my Mhlabelo root and squeezed some of its juice into the pot. Just as I had done this the three men re-entered the hut, one of them carrying a large pot of beer. This he put down in the middle of the floor, then turning to me he said: 'Thief, we have caught you today. You deny that you are a thief. The horses are evidence against you; we need no further proof. Tomorrow we will take you and the horses to our Chief, who will know how to deal with you.' This man then poured beer into the small drinking-pot and handed it to one of his companions, who drank deeply, handing the pot round to the others after he had drunk. They then began to argue as to which of them should keep guard over me. At last one said: 'As for me I am going to sleep; you others do as you will.' He had hardly finished speaking when he fell asleep, snoring, and a moment or two later the others were also fast asleep. My Mhlabelo was working nicely.

It was now late in the night. Making sure that the men were fast asleep, I slipped out of the hut and went to the cattle-fold where I found my horses. I took them out and mounting one I rode into the darkness. As soon as I was out of hearing I raced along until I came to the Umzintlanga River. I rode into the water with the three horses, then for a long time made my way downstream. The water was not deep, but travelling was very

56

rough. The horses stumbled and floundered along. After I had gone down the river for quite a considerable distance I came to a place where I thought I might leave it. I dismounted and tying the three horses to a tree by the water's edge – the horses being still in the water – I tore my blanket in half. I placed one half on the bank and led one of the horses on to it; then I placed the other half-blanket in front of the horse and led him on to that and so on, the horse always treading on the blanket as it went forward. I tied this horse up and returned for the other two, which I dealt with in a similar manner. I was quite satisfied that no spoor had been left. Then I made my way back to the kraal of the three men who had arrested me. I got there just as dawn was breaking. I crept into the hut and found the men still deep in slumber. I myself lay down and being tired out was asleep in a moment.

I woke to find that the sun was well up, shining through the chinks in the door.

One of the men woke and seemed relieved to see that I was there. He waked his companions. They all seemed to be in quarrelsome mood. One said: 'The beer of this kraal is an insult to the stomach of any man. I feel sick and my head aches so that it might split.' The second man said he also felt ill. The third man, the one who had brought the beer, said: 'The fault is with your own stomachs, not with my beer.' (My Mhlabelo had no doubt caused his head to ache as much as those of the other two.) 'You men go drinking from kraal to kraal, and when you come to me, sodden with intsipos (dregs) you have swallowed at other places, you blame my beer for your sore heads, Mawo!'

I here said: 'You men say I am a thief – your thief – and that you are going to take me to your Chief. Bring my horses and let us be going. As for me I have a long journey before me, and you have wasted enough of my time.'

The men got up and went outside, leaving me in the hut. After a little while they returned, regarding me with puzzled looks. I said: 'Come on, men; let us be going.'

One said: 'Where are the horses?'

I said: 'What horses?'

He replied: 'The horses with which we found you yesterday.'

I said: 'That is for you to know. You took them from me and put them in your kraal. They must still be there.' He replied that the horses had disappeared.

Then I sprang up as if in a great rage. I said: 'If you do not produce my horses at once, I will report the matter to your Chief and to the Magistrate. Dumezweni is a friend of mine and will know how to deal with you.'

One of the men said in a threatening manner: 'Do you talk like that, thief; we will take you to the Chief.'

I said: 'Take me to your Chief! And accuse me of what?'

He said, in a rather feeble way: 'We will charge you with the theft of three horses.'

At this I spat. 'Take me to your Chief without evidence! You talk like so many uncircumcised boys.'

These men knew full well that the Chief would not listen to them unless they produced the horses, and I knew that they would not dare to take me to him without them. They organised a search party and easily followed the spoor to the river. They searched up and down both banks, but could not find the place where the horses had left the water. They searched the whole day in vain.

Late in the afternoon they returned, looking crestfallen. I said: 'People of this kraal, I now require that my horses be handed over to me, otherwise it will be the worse for you. I have been stopped on my journey and my things have been taken from me. You say the horses are lost. I say they have been stolen and you are the thieves. I will report the matter to your Chief, and when he finds that this is a kraal of thieves he will cause it to be wiped out.'

The three men who had arrested me looked uneasily at each other. One said: 'Do not speak in that angry fashion; let us go into a hut and talk the thing quietly and without heat.'

We went into a hut. Beer was brought. I was glad to notice that it was handed round in a vessel other than the one that had been used the night before.

I repeated my claim to the horses. I knew that these people would not dare to bring the matter before the Chief for fear that they themselves might be accused of theft. I knew more-over that what they feared more than anything would be the ridicule of the men who would say: 'You arrest a man with stolen horses, and you lose the horses after having impounded them; what sort of people are you?'

After very much talk, of which I made it appear I was becoming weary, I said: 'You people have caused me to lose my three horses. I do not say you have stolen them, that is as may be. If you have stolen them, you must produce them. If you have lost them you must recover them. To show you that I do not wish to bring trouble upon people who up to now have been strangers to me, I am prepared to accept from you £10 as security for the production of the horses.'

The men objected to this, so I said the only thing to be done was to take the matter to the Chief. They asked me not to be hasty and requested me to withdraw from the hut while they considered the matter. I went out. After a while they called me in and said they were prepared to give me a cow as security. I said: 'What have I to do with your cows? Do you think that I want to be arrested again, perhaps by your own people, for being in possession of one of your cows? What explanation can I give in regard to a cow come by in this manner?'

After much talk these men offered to give me £5 as security. They said they were sure they would be able to recover the horses, and that they would bring them to our place within a few days and claim the return of their £5.

After some hesitation I agreed to accept the £5, which they handed to me. 'But,' I said, 'you people have done a thing which will cause me to walk. I came here mounted. Am I to go on foot to my home, which is far distant?'

After more talk these men agreed to lend me a horse. I said this horse should be included in the security for the production of my three horses. They were angry at first, but when I offered to return them their £5 and stated I was quite prepared to take the whole matter to the Chief they agreed that the horse should be included in the security.

They fetched the horse and I rode off well satisfied. I went to the place where I had left my three horses tethered to the roots of a thorn tree in a deep donga. I watered them and allowed them to graze for a while, and then as dusk fell I made for home.

I reached home in the very early hours of the morning, at first cockcrow. I told my father what had transpired, showed him the borrowed horse and handed him the £5.

When I woke up next morning it was already late. I went to see my father, but was informed that he was away having gone 'to his places'. I noticed that the four horses were no longer at our kraal.

The three men who had arrested me never came to claim their security, and the only thing that I ever heard of that matter was that when Ntuku went to visit them to learn what had transpired he was given a bad thrashing and driven away from their kraal.

12

Two Journeys to Qaukeni in the Pondo Country

My father returned after an absence of about a week. He brought with him four fine cattle which he said he had bought in a distant part of the country. He drove these cattle into the kraal and they went out with our cattle to graze. No questions were ever asked in regard to them.

It was about this time that my father called me to his hut. He announced that he was feeling old age coming upon him, and that he felt himself unable to undertake the long and arduous journeys his occupation required of him. He told me much of the people with whom he had been associated in distant parts. He mentioned kraals in remote places where I would always receive a welcome; he described to me side-paths and short cuts seldom used by other people, and he told me of certain places in different parts of the country in which horses or cattle might be placed where they would not be likely to be noticed.

He said that after my experience with the three men who had arrested me it would be as well to have someone to accompany me on expeditions such as that. He mentioned Nyaniso as a suitable companion. I was very pleased at this, for though Nyaniso and I had been friends from boyhood and had been in the same lodge at the time of our initiation into manhood, there were certain of our private family affairs which I had not mentioned to him, though I had often wished to speak to him of them.

I at once went over to Nyaniso's place and told him of my father's suggestion. I also told him of the different matters of business upon which I had recently been engaged. He said that his father had for many years been associated with mine in similar transactions.

It was finally arranged that Nyaniso should pay a visit to our kraal in order that he might share with me any instruction that my father saw fit to impart.

It was said that there was an extraordinary resemblance between Nyaniso and myself. When apart we were often mistaken for each other. This caused us amusement. To make the resemblance more close we wore bead ornaments of the same kind, blankets of similar description, our sticks were alike and we imitated each other's voices.

One evening after Nyaniso had been with us some days my father called us into his hut.

He said, as if telling us news: 'There is a man in the Pondo country named Kohlakali. He lives down in Qaukeni and is very rich. The kraal of this man is near the Gosa Forest. He has many cattle nqomaed with (lent to) people round about him but the best of his cattle he keeps at his own kraal. In the springtime they graze round about on the outskirts of the forest where the grass has been burnt and where it has begun to spring. That is where the cattle will be found at this time.'

Neither of us knew the Qaukeni country, and we said so; all we knew was that it was towards the sea-coast.

My father said that seawater was a well-known cure for certain ailments if used in a proper way. He felt that if he could get some seawater it would do him great good.

This was enough for us. We were to go down to the coast, announcing that we desired to fetch seawater for medicine, and on our way we observed Kohlakali's kraal, and certain other places of which we had been told.

We went to the coast and returned with the seawater. We had carefully observed Kohlakali's kraal without being noticed. We had seen the cattle, and had come to certain conclusions regarding them and had made our plans.

On a certain day we returned to the Qaukeni country and made our way to the neighbourhood of Kohlakali's kraal. There were the cattle grazing near the forest; three herdboys were in charge of them.

By arrangement Nyaniso went boldly up to the herdboys; he said: 'Is there any one of you boys who can climb a tree?' The boys said: 'Climb a tree for what?' Nyaniso said: 'Climb a tree for something sweet?' The boys asked: 'Sweet like what?' Nyaniso said: 'Sweet like honey. I have found a bees' nest in a tree, but I was never good at climbing, having lived in a country where trees are few. You fellows who live near a forest of trees should be able to climb well.'

Two of the boys said they would try and climb the tree; the third said he would remain in charge of the cattle. We had expected something like this, and were prepared for it.

After Nyaniso had been gone for some time I approached the boy who had been left with the cattle, and while at a distance from him shouted imitating Nyaniso's voice: 'Heyi, you fellow sitting there, do you allow your companions to be stabbed by bees while they get honey which you will eat? Come to our aid. The bees are enraged and the nest is fat with honey.'

The boy jumped up and came towards me. I darted off into the bush, shouting to him to follow. I crouched behind a fallen tree and hid while the boy passed me thinking I was still in front of him. He ran on, and when I heard him shouting to try and find out where his companions were I went to the herd of cattle. I selected three of the best animals and made off with them.

I could hear the boys shouting to each other in the forest, but could not make out what they said. I skirted the forest for a while, then came out into open country. Here I drove the cattle as fast as they could go. I came to a deep valley where there was thick bush and drove the cattle into it, then I went up to a place from which I could see the surrounding country. In the distance I saw Nyaniso coming towards me. I signalled to him to show him where the cattle were in the bush, and made him understand that he was to drive them on.

I sat for quite a long while at this place, and as dusk was beginning to fall I espied a number of men armed with sticks and assegais who seemed to be following up the spoor of the cattle I had taken from Kohlakali's herd. When the men got to near the spot where I had driven the cattle into the bush I rose up and began to run. The men saw me and I heard one of them shout: 'There he is; there is the thief; catch him.' The three herds were with the men and they shouted that they recognised me as the man who had led them into the bush in search of a bees' nest. I ran and kept on running in a direction different from that which I knew Nyaniso would take. The men pursued me, seeming to be more anxious to capture a supposed thief than to recover their cattle. They thought no doubt if they caught the thief the recovery of the cattle would follow.

It was becoming dark now. The men pursuing me extended themselves in a long line. There was hardly light enough for them to see me. Just then I came to a bush lying in a kloof with steep sides. I quickly rolled a stone down the steep side of the kloof. I heard one of them shout: 'We have him; we have him; he's jumped down a krantz into the bush; surround the bush!'

When I heard what the men said, I turned in a different direction and darting behind a patch of bush I saw the men coming up in such manner as to make it clear that they intended to surround the small bush into which I had rolled the stone.

It was dark by now. I turned back and went in the very direction from which I had come. I could hear the men shouting to each other as they surrounded the bush. They seemed to be sure I was in hiding there. As I went on my way the sounds of shouting grew fainter, and then no longer reached my ears. I ran on at a steady pace for a long time, making for a place on the Camtsholo Ridge that Nyaniso and I knew of, where there was a deep gorge running down to the Umzintlanga River. There I found Nyaniso and the cattle.

We rested there that night, taking it in turns to keep watch. Just as the grey of dawn showed we went on our way. After a while we separated: I made for my father's kraal, while Nyaniso went on with the cattle making for a place of which my father had told us.

13

A Business Visit to Basutoland and its Outcome

I reported to my father what had transpired, when he gave me instructions as to the disposal of the three cattle. We were to take them across the Drakensberg into Basutoland; we were to travel by a particular route, which my father explained, along which we would find kraals at certain places where the people would be friendly. After crossing the Basutoland boundary at a particular spot we would soon come to the kraal of a man named Mohadi, who would instruct us how to proceed. I rejoined Nyaniso and we went on our way. We took it in turns to drive the cattle. While one drove, the other kept well in front so as to send back a signal if any suspicious people were encountered. So we proceeded till we reached the foothills of the Drakensberg, where we came to one of the friendly kraals of which my father had spoken. This kraal was in a very rugged place: great boulders sheltered it and below it was a krantz; above it stood the Drakensberg, by far the greatest mountains I had ever seen; their peaks appeared to pierce the sky.

At this kraal the people seemed to know all about us and they were very friendly. The head of the kraal was a Baphuti man named Morosi. He asked after the health of my father, with whom, from the conversation, it appeared he had had many dealings. Morosi instructed his son Lesalla to accompany us into Basutoland, as he knew every path and bypath over the mountains.

We left Morosi's kraal at dawn the next morning, taking a

slender track which led up and up and still up. At some places it was so narrow that if our cattle had made a single false step they would have fallen and would still be falling while you could count ten. Lesalla knew the difficulties of these paths, and with his aid we were able to get our cattle to the top of the mountains.

From there Lesalla told us to look back. Away very far down below we could see clusters of huts that looked like so many little brown ticks, roads looked like songololos (centipedes) and streams looked like strands of white cotton.

We passed on, and when the sun was well up we arrived at the kraal of Mohadi.

This man surprised us. He spoke to us in Sesuto, which we did not understand, then he spoke to us in our own language. He asked us many rude questions which were difficult to answer: 'What are you Matabeles[1] doing at my kraal? Whose cattle are these that you are driving? Are you running away from the police?' Before we had even time to offer any explanation Mohadi told us to be gone, and with this he retired into his hut.

Being in a strange country and among strange people, we began to fear for our safety and we looked to Lesalla for guidance. He said it was not for him to question the ways of old men, which were not always as easy as young men might wish, but he would reason with Mohadi and endeavour to find out what was in his mind.

Lesalla left us and entered the old man's hut. As soon as he was gone the women of the kraal came to us and told us to be gone. They said we were bringing their place, which had ever borne a good name, into disrepute. We asked in what way we had done this. They said we had come to their place

---

[1] The Basuto generally refer to the Sixhosa-speaking people as 'Matabeles'.

with cattle. Whence had we obtained these cattle? Whose were they? Why had we brought them there?

We were dumb. In our country it was not the custom for women to question the actions of grown men. We knew not what next to do or say, but just then Mohadi and Lesalla reappeared and the women withdrew themselves.

Mohadi addressed us: 'Are you youths adding to the affronts you have offered to my place by interfering with its women? What do you mean by your conduct? Are you an impi come to steal the cattle and women of a peaceable people?'

We were astounded. We had done no wrong to the women of Mohadi's place, we had offered affront to no man or woman there; but yet we had a bad feeling. We Xesibes were in a strange country, we knew not the usages of this place, we might innocently have done a thing most displeasing to the people. All these thoughts passed through our minds much more quickly than they are spoken.

Then Mohadi spoke again: 'You young men from a distant place, it may be that I have judged you hastily and without giving you full hearing. Come into the nkundla (courtyard) and give an account of yourselves in my presence and before the men of this place.'

We suspected Lesalla of treachery; he sat still beside Mohadi, saying nothing, and we thought he had arrayed himself with those who appeared to be our enemies. For a short space there was silence, then one of the older men addressing Nyaniso and myself said: 'You two young men, from the Matabele country, have you nothing to say for yourselves?'

It was hastily agreed between Nyaniso and myself that I should speak. I said: 'Men of this place, we are strangers to you, as your people and country are strange to us. If through ignorance we have done what to you appears unseemly, we will withdraw, and in token of good faith we will leave you with the cattle we have brought with us. Our fathers led us to understand that the people of this place were his friends; if it be otherwise, tell us so, and we will know that we are intruders and as speedily as may be return whence we have come.'

Nyaniso and I had but our sticks with us; these we grasped firmly, expecting that we should have to defend ourselves against these people who seemed anxious to be at enmity with us. We were of a people who had from all time stood upon the defensive; it was thus not for us to submit without reason to a false position thrust upon us. We observed that at this stage some of the older men smiled, but yet we held ourselves ready for what might befall.

Then stood up old Mohadi and said: 'These lads from a distant place seem ready to take offence where none has been intended. As they should know, had they been properly in-structed, our banter was intended merely as a test to induce them to show their hardihood and prove that they were worthy of those from whose places they alleged they have come. Let us go into a more private place and speak more intimately of those things with which these young men appear to be concerned.'

So saying, Mohadi led the way into his hut; the other older men followed. Nyaniso and I were the last to enter, and as strangers and subordinates sat down near the left-hand side of the entrance. Leting (Basuto beer) was handed round in a clay pot, such a pot as we had never before seen; its sides were smooth and shiny and it was beautifully fashioned. Surely these Basuto were skilled in the making of pots.

The beer-pot was first placed before Mohadi, who said a few words in Sesuto, which we could not understand; then referring to Nyaniso and myself he said in our own language: 'These two young men are children of the friends of my childhood, manhood and old age; their fathers have been as

69

my own brothers; in this place, what there is is theirs.'

This speech of Mohadi surprised and pleased us, but as Lesalla yet sat still suspicion remained in our minds. I nevertheless said: 'Mohadi, my Chief, my father directed me to you on a matter of business. I was told that this place was one where dwelt friends of his, thus are we here. If my father has been mistaken, release us and let us go.'

Mohadi's reply was: 'Child of my old friend, you have spoken as would your own father.'

From this time on no particular notice was taken of Nyaniso and myself; we were not slighted, yet nor was special attention paid to us. Late that evening a sleeping-place was provided for us, and notwithstanding our misgivings weariness soon brought us to sleep.

We were out before dawn to see to our cattle. They were not in the kraal where we had placed them! We went to look for Lesalla and could not find him. On enquiring as to his whereabouts, we were told that he had 'gone to his places'. We felt that our suspicions had been well founded and that these Basuto had stolen our cattle from us. We knew not what next to do. At that time old Mohadi emerged from his hut wrapped in his kaross with his cat-skin cap drawn over his head. He saw us and at once fell into a rage. Addressing us he said: 'Are you two uncircumcised boys come to question the ways of this kraal? Did not your fathers say that friends were here, and yet you two crawl around upon your bellies like a couple of scorpions seeking to bring ill and do ill. Get back to your sleeping-places, lest I call out the women and girls to thrash you!'

We went back to the hut that had been set apart for us, marvelling at the ways of the Basuto. We felt ourselves in evil case, and if we did take our rest we would be in no worse plight; so we slept. We left things to take their own course in this strange country.

We were wakened later by a knock at the door. We opened, when a young boy bearing a pot of beer entered. He placed the pot before us and withdrew without a word. We partook of the beer, feeling as we did so that if we were in evil plight a little beer would make our situation no worse.

After the sun had risen we arose, went outside and sat against the hut-wall in the sunlight. After a while old Mohadi reappeared and sat beside us. He said to us: 'You lads are young and have much to learn; moreover, you appear to have been improperly instructed. Your fathers, you tell me, said you were to come to this place; do you not trust your fathers? Why then should you be suspicious of people whom your fathers trusted? Is that not an insult to us and a reproach to your own people? If any untoward thing befall you at this kraal or as the result of your having been here, upon my head be it.' So saying, he withdrew.

I looked at Nyaniso, who returned my gaze; we both laughed and realised that we were foolish fellows.

Later in the day a goat was slaughtered; we ate of the meat and made merry, old Mohadi seeming to be much pleased that we had accepted the ways of his kraal and people, as indeed we had.

Late that evening Lesalla appeared with three fine horses. He was very weary. He came straight up to Nyaniso and myself and said: 'Here are your three cows which you suspected me of stealing; take your things, so that you may no longer cherish suspicion against me in your hearts.' We begged Lesalla to retire with us into a hut so that we might learn from him more of the ways of his people and not again be found at fault on account of our ignorance.

Lesalla made plain much that had puzzled us. He told us that our people and his own for very many years past had had transactions in the course of which cattle had been brought from our country and exchanged for horses in his. The basis of all these transactions had been implicit trust between his people and our own. They questioned not our methods and expected no question from us. One man worked one way, another worked differently. It was now not for us to enquire as to whence he had acquired the horses – he had not questioned us as to whence the cattle had come. So for a while we conversed about matters of this kind till full mutual understanding and friendship was established between us. I was very glad of this, the more so as I had noticed the sister of Lesalla who was good to look upon, a young woman of marriageable age who spoke with a melodious voice and who had a ready smile. I noticed moreover that she busied herself with the household affairs of her father's kraal, ordering all things well. She looked strong and healthy, fit mother for a man's children.

After Lesalla had retired I mentioned to Nyaniso something of what had been in my mind regarding this girl. Nyaniso listened with becoming sympathy to what I said and undertook, should I seriously think of marriage, to make advances on my behalf when the time came. I was not sure whether this would be quite suitable, as Nyaniso was a fine-looking young man and, as I have said, very like me in appearance. There was time enough to consider these matters, as we still had to complete our business with the horses, and I would have to consult my father in the matter of marriage.

As Nyaniso and I made our way homewards with the horses, the one thing in my mind was the thought of marriage. Young women had not up to now interested me. This one was of a different people; how would my father regard the matter? As for me, differences of clan or custom were as nothing – this was the maiden of my fancy. I knew full well that it would be regarded as unusual for a man of the Xesibe to mate with an Msutu maiden. Would my father consent to the marriage and pay the dowry? I ceased to think of the horses; I could think only of the girl Mokhoatsi.

Nyaniso endeavoured to engage me in conversation; from what he said it seemed that I answered him foolishly. Suddenly he said: 'We are being followed; danger is behind us.' I looked back and saw that horsemen were following us. Hastily we agreed that in case of extremity each should act independently of the other. We urged on our horses to their full speed, but they had come a long way and would not be able to last long. Our pursuers were gaining upon us. I thought of a plan which I conveyed to Nyaniso in a few hasty words. I would throw myself off my horse, making it appear as if I had fallen. Nyaniso would at the same time jump off the horse he was riding and mount the third which would still be fresh. I would make off into rough country where I might be able to elude our pursuers till darkness set in, when escape would be easy. We concluded that those who followed would endeavour to capture me, and having done so would be able, through me, to find out the identity of my companion and destination of the horses. Nyaniso disagreed with this plan, but I insisted that in it lay our only hope of safety. We slackened our pace. I made it appear as if I were reeling in my seat, and then flung myself from my horse. At the same moment Nyaniso jumped from his horse, mounted the third and raced off with the two we had been riding. I made for a rugged hillside where there were boulders and bush. As we had expected, the men – there were three – made after me. I felt that I would not be able to keep on running for very long in this rough country, but I noticed that the men had had to slacken their pace.

Suddenly I came upon a kraal. I noticed that though it was the evening hour no fires were burning; the owners must be away. My breath was failing; I was becoming utterly exhausted and the men were gaining upon me. I rushed up to the nearest hut, dragged open the wicker door and entered. Sticking in the thatch of the roof I found an assegai. I grasped this and waited for what might befall, having thrust the door to. I heard the men dash up on their horses and I heard what was said: 'Now we have him; he cannot escape us.' Another, agreeing, said: 'We have him caged like a trapped monkey; all we have to do is wait until it is our time to take him out, then we'll make him dance in front of the Chief.' The third said: 'Let's go and stir him up and see what kind of a thief this is who has given us such a run.' They all seemed pleased with themselves. One said: 'Where are the people of this kraal? Since we have caught a thief here, it is only right that they should provide us with refreshment.' Thereupon one went off, apparently to see what he could find in the store hut. After a short while he returned, announcing that he had found a large pot of beer, the children having informed him that their parents had gone to a beer drink at a distant place.

Through the chinks in the door I could see these three fellows sitting in front of the hut, the beer-pot passing from one to another. I would have given a fat heifer for one deep draught from that pot.

These men sat and drank beer and talked and smoked till it was dark and time for me to make my escape if that were possible. I thought that bold action would be my only course.

I said: 'Ho, you fellows without, why do you not come inside and share with me the comforts this hut provides?' After a short pause, which showed me they were surprised, one said: 'Be quiet, thief; it is not fit that we should share a hut with a thief; besides, we here without have sufficient comforts to keep us cheerful.' I said: 'Let us all be cheerful together, sharing the comforts this hospitable kraal provides.' One replied: 'There are no comforts for you, thief, other than those that may be found in the tails of ikatsi (cat-o'-nine tails).'

I said, thinking the while of Mokhoatsi: 'If you riff-raff are not coming in to talk with me, I will go out and go about my business.' They laughed at this and spoke among themselves in a way disparaging to me. This annoyed me and, thinking of how Mokhoatsi might applaud bold action on my part should she hear of it, I said: 'You common fellows sitting in a kraal which does not belong to you drinking beer which you have stolen, I am now going on my way, I do not wish to be found with petty pilferers of beer.' The men laughed at this. I suddenly flung open the hut door, shouting, 'Look out! I'm off for my home now.' As I said this the three men jumped up and stood ready for me outside the hut; two had assegais and one had sticks. In the hut I had found a large pot. I wrapped my blanket around this. I shouted: 'Look out! I'm coming!' As I shouted I flung out the pot, two assegais penetrated the blanket, one stick smashed the pot, and as these several weapons were down I dashed out; smiting left and right with my stick, I bounded into the darkness and so away among the bush and boulders.

The owner of that kraal had done me no harm, so I dropped the assegai I had found in the hut soon after leaving the kraal. I heard the three men giving each other orders; I heard them rush for their horses; I heard them start off in pursuit, but by that time I was lost to them in the darkness.

Having thoroughly rested while in the hut, I felt fresh and it was pleasant in the cool night air. I ran on with a long, steady stride. The men had gone in a direction they thought I would take, but I had kept up higher on the mountainside among the bush and boulders. I kept on running at a steady pace till about midnight, then rested for a while at a stream, where I refreshed myself drinking deeply from its icy water. In a quiet pool I saw the reflection of the stars – how like the eyes of Mokhoatsi, thought I.

After resting for a while I continued my way, running at a steady pace. I knew that Nyaniso would make for a certain kraal where there were friends, and wait for me there after secreting the horses. I made for this kraal, reaching its neighbourhood after the sun was well up. I remained at a distance on a little hillock where I might observe the movements of the people. I saw three horses there that looked like the horses of the men who had pursued us, and I feared that these men might have caught Nyaniso. I lay in hiding for a long time, seeing but not seen, then I saw three men appear from a hut, followed by Nyaniso and a man whom I knew to be the head of the kraal. A boy was sent to catch the three horses I had seen, and the men mounted and rode off. After waiting till these men were well out of sight, I came down from out my hiding-place and made for the hut which Nyaniso and Kupiso, the head of the kraal, had re-entered. Nyaniso greeted me joyfully; Kupiso smote me in a friendly way on the back, and laughed and kept on laughing. He ordered beer to be brought. I knew not the cause of his laughter, but each of us would tell his tale in good time.

Beer was brought and placed before us. When I saw the beer-pot I thought to myself what poor makers of pots we were; the Basuto were much more skilled in the art of pot-making than we. I wondered what part of the work of making earthen vessels was undertaken by Mokhoatsi. I felt sure that she would be able to fashion a beautiful vessel; her fingers were long and her hands well shaped, she would mould the clay in graceful pattern.

These thoughts were interrupted by Kupiso, who asked me to give an account of what had happened to me. After I had told him he smote me upon the back and laughed; he laughed so heartily that I began to think that he had had more beer than is good for a man.

Then Nyaniso told me his story. Directly he had seen that

I had not been injured by the fall from my horse, he had mounted the third horse, making off with all speed, leading the other two. He had seen the three men turn off in pursuit of me and had seen me make for the rough ground. He said he knew I was like a coney when among stones. He, losing sight of me, pressed on at the utmost speed for Kupiso's kraal. As soon as he had secreted the horses, he asked Kupiso to give him a place to sleep. Kupiso wanted him to sit up and talk, but he refused, saying he must lie down and sleep at once. A rush mat was brought and Nyaniso lay down upon it, wrapping himself in his blanket. Kupiso sat by the fire and smoked. Nyaniso said that before long it might be seen why he was so anxious to be asleep. Kupiso sat by the fire and smoked and kept on smoking, the only sound to be heard being the hiss of his spittle as it met the coals of the fire. After a very long time voices were heard without and then someone said: 'Nqo! nqo! nqo![2] May we enter?' Kupiso got up and opened the hut door, asking who might be there. Three men with sweating horses said: 'We have been chasing thieves; one has eluded us on foot, the other made off with three horses and he may have come this way. Have you seen a person of such and such a description passing this way?' The description was such as might have applied either to Nyaniso or myself. They said that they had the blanket of the thief who had been on foot. Their account of my escape was that they had been so close upon my heels they had grasped my blanket. I had dropped it, causing them to trip and fall, so had I made my escape. They produced the blanket. Kupiso handled it, saying, 'Kwowu! If we only had the fellow who should be inside this, we would have a thief. Give me this blanket as intlonze (evidence) and I'll find the thief for you.'

---

[2] Symbolic knocking.

It was at this stage that Nyaniso stirred, stretched himself and yawned. 'What is all this talk of thieves?' said he, as he coughed and spat as one waking from heavy sleep.

As he showed his face in the firelight the three men closed upon him, saying, 'This is he, this is our thief; hand him over to us.' Kupiso said: 'Go slow, young men, go slow. I am no harbourer of thieves; this young man is my guest, any accusation brought against him reflects upon me. I know him to be an honest man. He has been at my kraal this long time, has supped with me, has lodged with me, so that he is an inmate of this kraal for whom I am responsible. I vouch for him.'

'But we have his blanket, here it is,' said the men.

Then Nyaniso, once more yawning and stretching himself, sat up in his resting-place and gazed with sleep-sodden eyes at the three men. 'What is this talk of thieves and blankets?' said he. 'This blanket which now enwraps me was purchased for money at the store of a white storekeeper who is well known for honest dealing. Is it the blanket of a kind that might be lent by the honourable head of a kraal to a casual visitor?'

'Blankets may be so and so,' said one of the men. 'Blankets may be speedily changed, but a man's face is his for his lifetime and there are no changes upon it except such as age may bring. We had but a fleeting glance of this young man's face, but we are not mistaken in him. It is he who shed his blanket at our feet, causing us to stumble; it is he who, making away with the horses of our people, was by providence caused to fall from his horse.'

Kupiso said: 'Call any member of this kraal and question him or her, be it man or woman, as to this young man's movements, as to the manner of his arrival at this kraal mounted or afoot, as to whether he came clothed or without a blanket; question my people, and if upon any point they disagree with what I have told you, take this young man and do with him as seems to you meet.'

It had not been expected, but these men first roused the small children of the place. As is well known, the children of a kraal are the most observant of its people. They notice all that transpires, but being innocent and ignorant of the ways of grown men they do not discuss these matters among themselves, but merely store them in the granaries of their minds as mealies are stored in a pit till such time as they are required for use.

Being questioned, the children said that Nyaniso had arrived at the kraal just about the time the cattle were being brought in, he was mounted and rode at an ordinary pace, being in no great haste; he had on the blanket he was now wearing.

The children had answered discreetly, and on the morrow they would be given meat to eat.

The three men, not being satisfied with the answers of the children, roused the women and questioned them. They answered in the same strain as the children. This gave the men pause, and the women being quick to notice an advantage began to question them. 'You youths who have disturbed us, who are you and whence do you come? Is it not possible that you know more about these horses than you are prepared to disclose? Are you not perhaps trying to thrust upon this kraal guilt which you yourselves should carry?'

Here Kupiso intervened. He called the men into his hut and gave orders for a goat to be slaughtered. He questioned the men as to the description of the three horses. He said that a strange man had been at the kraal and had mentioned in the course of conversation that he had seen a man riding a horse and leading two others. A full description of the horses had not been given, as they were not of any particular interest, but it might be these were the missing horses. He did not know where the strange man lived, but he mentioned that he was going to Umsikaba. He had seen the man with the three horses near Centuli; no doubt if enquiries were made in that neighbourhood something might be found out. He asked the three men to have some of the meat of the goat. While they were eating he said that the more he thought of it the more he was convinced that the man he had heard of with the three horses was the man for whom they were looking.

Kupiso kept the three men at his kraal for quite a while. He had meantime sent off a young man to Centuli, who was instructed to keep a watch upon the path the three men would take. When he saw them approaching he would show himself as travelling in the opposite way to that the men would be taking; he would, if asked as to his business, say he was in search of a stray ox, and when questioned, as he was sure to be, whether he had seen a man with three horses he was to say he certainly had seen a man riding a horse and leading two others. He would be in some doubt as to the description of the three horses, but when the men described them he was to be sure that the horses he had seen were those of which the men were in search. He would be asked to describe the person in charge of the three horses and would give a vague description of myself which would be sufficient for the men to recognise.

Kupiso, on one pretext and another, detained the men at his kraal as long as he could, but at last they asked to be excused and thanking Kupiso for his proffered assistance they went about their business. The young man who had been sent to intercept them returned later, reporting that he had met them and given them information upon which they had decided to go down towards Qaukeni, which was several days' journey from Kupiso's kraal.

The three men after some time returned to Kupiso, reporting that they had not found the horses. They stated that they had met a young man who had actually seen the thief with the horses, that they had gone on in a direction indicated by the young man, and though they had made many and searching enquiries they had found no further trace of the thief or the horses.

Kupiso expressed his sympathy with the men in their loss, and said he would continue to make enquiries and if he met with any success he would inform the men by means of a messenger whom he undertook to send to them.

Those men never saw their horses again.

14

Disappointment

All these days I had been thinking of Mokhoatsi away in her home on the Drakensberg. After we had properly disposed of the three horses I asked Nyaniso if he could not accompany me to her father's kraal and make overtures of marriage on my behalf. At first he refused flatly to go. He kept on asking whether there were not girls of our own people from whom I might choose. I replied as often that there was no girl for me but Mokhoatsi, so in the end it was arranged that we should go and propose marriage to her people, my father reluctantly giving his consent.

On a day we started out on our journey, wearing our best beads and blankets and carrying presents for Mokhoatsi's parents.

In due course we arrived at Morosi's kraal, where we found a gathering of people. We were very soon informed as to what was going on: the people of the young man to whom Mokhoatsi was betrothed had brought dowry cattle! This was the first I had heard of Mokhoatsi's betrothal and I was struck dumb by the news. I felt as if I had been taken unawares and smitten with a bunguza (heavy knobbed stick). After a while Nyaniso called me aside; he said: 'I am sorry for you, my brother, in this thing that has befallen you. Remember that you are a man of the Xesibe; show a brave face and leave the talking to me.' I was glad to agree to this, as I had no words.

There was much beer, and meat was plentiful. All the people were in joyful mood; it seemed to me that I alone was sorrowful.

When the matter of dowry came to be discussed Nyaniso and I took our places among the men. After the talk was finished and beer was passing round, Nyaniso spoke when a suitable opportunity offered. Addressing Morosi, he said: 'My Chief, friend of our fathers, we from the Xesibe country had heard that this betrothal ceremony was to take place on this day. Your name is well known in distant places, so it is that news of the affairs of this your kraal is carried far afield. We, having heard of the great thing that is to happen today, are here, though uninvited. We have journeyed far and fast, so that people from our place might be present to wish you well. Our fathers are old men, otherwise they themselves would be amongst you. They bade us say that their wishes in this matter are what your own may be. May good fortune follow your children.'

This speech of Nyaniso surprised me; it was of something I did not know. As he sat down he trod very heavily upon my foot and whispered: 'Xesibe man, say that it is so.'

I sprang up as my foot was trodden on and caught Nyaniso's words as I rose. I had in reality nothing to say, but being upon my feet in the face of the seated assemblage I must say something. I remembered that Nyaniso had said nothing of the presents we had brought. I said, speaking thickly: 'My Chief, we have brought with us a few small gifts in token of our good wishes; if for one moment you will excuse my friend and myself, we will fetch them.' I withdrew, followed closely by Nyaniso, who said I had spoken stoutly. He added to this other words of encouragement.

Returning, I placed before Morosi a neatly patterned sleeping-mat, two meat mats, in the making of which our people are skilled, a beer strainer the like of which I was sure these people had never seen, and sundry other articles which anyone might be proud to receive as complimentary gifts.

'These poor gifts,' said I, 'are in earnest of what my companion has spoken. We have come from a distant place, but even there the affairs of this kraal become known to us, thus we are here. Accept from us these trifling things and with them receive the good wishes of our people. May this marriage be prosperous and may good fortune attend parents and children.' As I sat down, I felt that strength had gone from me; I was weak as water. I had seen Mokhoatsi at a distance, but I had always endeavoured to throw my eyes in another direction when I saw her.

As I finished my speech and sat down, it was Nyaniso that caused me almost to spring up again; he again trod on my foot with force, at the same time whispering, 'Well spoken, Xesibe man, the worst is over.'

Old Morosi responded with cordiality to what we had said. He praised our presents, and said we were worthy sons of our fathers; we were to him as his own children, even as our fathers had been as his own brothers. He thanked us for the gifts we had brought and for our good wishes. What he said fell upon my dull ears. It was only long afterwards that Nyaniso reminding me I remembered what had been said.

The young man who was to be Mokhoatsi's husband was presented to us, and I am now able to say that he was a well-looking fellow, tall in stature and of pleasant appearance; but at that time I felt sorrow for the maid who was expected to mate with a man I regarded as but a sorry person.

Requesting the company to excuse us, as we had urgent affairs requiring our attention at our homes necessitating a very early departure in the morning, we withdrew, bidding farewell to all who had made us welcome.

I slept little that night, and it was before dawn that I roused Nyaniso, saying that it was time we were up and going. We left before the people of the kraal were astir, and for a long time we rode homewards in silence; then, as we saw the red of sunrise showing, Nyaniso said: 'Look, the sun is rising on a new day. Yesterday with its happenings is behind us; we are astride with the affairs of today. We are able to plan for the doings of tomorrow. Let us look forward.' I felt then that it was easy for him to talk in this strain, but as for me I had the day before been in high hope and happy mood and had now no wish to leave for ever behind me plans and scenes that had formed themselves so deeply and clearly in my inner mind. We rode on in silence. It was somehow borne in upon me that Nyaniso spoke truly, and I began to have the feeling that he was a *real* Xesibe man, of whose companionship one might be proud; so as we rode along silently, knee to knee, a new and indescribable feeling towards him arose in my breast.

When for a rest we halted and dismounted, I said to Nyaniso: 'My father's child, it seems to me that a bond between us has grown up on this journey the like of which I have not known between men. Your timely speech and ready action saved me from foolish indiscretion which might have brought us and our people into disrepute. When I first heard of the betrothal, I was prepared for any mad act which in the end would have wrought us broken pates if nothing worse.'

On our return home the news of our journey was conveyed to my father by Nyaniso; I could not bring myself to speak of it. My father received the intelligence gravely, his only remark to me being: 'My son, you are still a young man.'

15

An Escape and a Quarrel

For many days I kept to myself, refusing to take any part in the affairs of our kraal and taking no interest in the usual things that go to make up our life.

One day Nyaniso came to see me, and receiving no response to his friendly conversation he became angry. He said: 'You Xesibe man, are you for ever going to sit moping and blinking like an owl that has been driven into the sunlight? Come on, join us, and once more be one of us. I have brought you a medicine specially prepared by Kwanguba for ailments such as yours.'

I took the medicine, which caused me soon to be violently sick; after that my head ached as though it would split, so much so that I began to think more of my head than of Mokhoatsi. I asked Nyaniso what kind of poison was this with which he was killing me. He said: 'Have you no faith in the cures of Kwanguba? This is a strong medicine for a stubborn sickness. Tomorrow I'll bring you another medicine which will complete the cure; it will at the same time remove the pains from your head.'

In the morning I felt much better, and when I had taken the second medicine brought me by Nyaniso the pains in my head ceased and the feeling of deep depression left me.

Nyaniso told me that there was to be a dance for young people at a certain kraal that night, and mentioned in a casual way that some of his people would be there. He proposed that we should also go. I did not feel in the mood for dances and said so. Nyaniso left it at that.

Late that afternoon he returned to our kraal dressed up in the best of his finery, and I must say he looked well. I asked what was the meaning of this display. He said he was going to the dance of which he had told me in the morning. I asked where was his horse, as the place was far distant and he would not, going on foot, reach the dance in time. He said he was going to ride one of Madevu's two fine horses. I said that Madevu the trader was a friend of ours, but he would lend those two beautiful horses to no one. Nyaniso said he would nevertheless ride one of them and suggested that I should ride the other. After some talk I agreed, and then and there threw aside the pain that had been in my mind.

It was late in the afternoon, and as dusk fell we set out for Madevu's place. When we got there all was quiet. We saw lights burning in Madevu's house. We made our way cautiously to the stable and there found the two horses; one snorted and stamped as we entered the stable, but whistling quietly in a way we knew of soon put them at ease. We fastened their reins in their mouths and led them out. Once clear of the houses, we mounted, riding quietly; but as soon as we got away from the place we put those horses to their utmost speed – they were horses the like of which I had never before been astride. As we raced along a feeling of joyfulness and youth returned to me. Then I knew that Kwanguba's medicine had worked a full cure, I was once more myself. Had silence not been necessary, I should have shouted with joy. As it was, all I could do was to whistle softly in a way that horses know when one who likes them is upon their back. So we sped along.

We were still a long distance from the kraal where the dance was to take place, when Nyaniso said we should halt and put

87

ourselves in order. We tethered the horses so that they should be able to crop the grass round about, and we put our dress in order so that people might conclude we had come afoot.

When we reached the kraal we found the dance to be in full progress. As we entered the dance hut we were hailed by our friends with hearty greetings, also with questionings as to the lateness of our arrival. We responded heartily to the greetings, and said we had arrived somewhat late owing to the appearance at my place of strangers upon whom we were required to attend.

Of the people at the dance most were our intimate friends in whose company we were glad to be, but there was one present who made me grasp my sticks – that was Ntuku the mole. One knew not where he might come up and what mischief he might not try to do. When I saw that he seemed to claim particular intimacy with the sister of Nyaniso, I grasped my sticks the firmer. What was Nyaniso doing in the matter? He seemed to take no notice – to be unconcerned in regard to the advances of a common fellow like Ntuku towards his sister. What surprised me was that a sister of my friend could even bear the company of such a fellow. She smiled at his would-be pleasantries, and as she did not repel his overtures there was that about her attitude towards him which must be displeasing in the eyes of her brother as it was distasteful to me, her brother's friend. Common folks do and say things in an offensive way; the same things may be done and said by a man of breeding without offence. If Nyaniso were to see nothing and do nothing, I would take the matter up. Was Nyaniso out of his senses that he did not observe the trend of things?

Nyaniso was meantime making merry after our fashion with this one, the other one and another. He was always well beloved in a company such as this. His sallies ever met with a ready laugh. His presence was looked for at any gathering of young people. He was beloved by all, in that he always caused those in his company to laugh. Above all he was sought after by old women, for whom he had always a kindly word and a witty saying which set their pendulant paps a-quivering with merriment.

I was not enjoying myself; I felt in quarrelsome mood. The affairs of the sister of Nyaniso had nothing to do with me but as her brother's friend I resented the manner in which Ntuku regarded and addressed her – to me, as a friend of her people, it was offensive. When would Nyaniso assert himself? I was hoping for the moment when one or the other of us would find it our duty to crack Ntuku's skull. An end was put to my desires in the matter by Nyaniso making his way over to where I sat in the hut and whispering that it was high time we returned Madevu's horses to their place. I followed him out of the hut, and by the time we got to the horses the grey dawn was showing. Without a word to Nyaniso I mounted my horse and raced off into the mist of early dawn. I had a feeling of greater hatred towards Ntuku than I thought he could ever have aroused, and for the moment I thought that Nyaniso had failed in his duty to his sister, so I raced off into the mist wishing that I might never see these people again. I smote Madevu's horse on the flank with one of my sticks in a way that caused him to bound and fly over the ground so that almost before I knew it I was at Madevu's place. A moment or two later Nyaniso came up. 'Kwowu, Xesibe man,' said he, 'you have ridden as if Tikoloshe (the water-sprite) were after you; the horses are wet with sweat, and it will be bad for them if they are put in the stable; let us leave them in the paddock.' I left my horse and strode off in the direction of home, not wishing to speak to any man, not even to Nyaniso. He soon overtook me.

'What now, Xesibe man?' said he. 'What ails you? Has the

medicine of Kwanguba taken a wrong turning or has someone done a thing that offends you?' He placed his hand on my shoulder, but I shook it off and turned on him. 'What sort of a brother are you,' I said, 'that you can leave your sister in the hands of such an evil fellow as Ntuku? You saw the way that things were going, yet you sat and took no notice. You continued to smile upon all as is your wont and cracked your feeble jokes while your sister was being entrapped by that evil fellow.'

The next I heard was a shout: 'Arm yourself! Are you insulting me and my people with your talk? Arm yourself and show if you *are* a Xesibe man. I have addressed you that way in affection; stand up and defend yourself or show yourself to be a Xesibe dog.'

In a moment we were engaged. Day was dawning and the light was sufficient. This was the very thing I wanted, to feel the thud of my induku upon the skull of someone, I cared not whose; so we watched and struck, parried and feinted, closed and broke away, always the clatter of stick upon stick. So we fought and kept on fighting. I could hear Nyaniso's hard breathing, as I felt he might hear mine. This was no boys' play, this was a fight; no pause for a rest, no halt to adjust sticks; it was to be a fight to a finish. Suddenly I heard and felt a crash; all the stars of the heavens gathered about my head, and I knew no more.

When I came to myself I found that I was in a hut. Nyaniso was bending over me, pressing to my lips some unpleasant liquid which he urged me to take. As I was consumed with a burning thirst, I drank it greedily, unpleasant as was its taste. I had felt a terrible pain in my head, but this became easier and I fell into a restful sleep.

When I awoke it was late in the afternoon. My mind was now clear and everything came back to me – Madevu's horses, the dance, the fight. I called to Nyaniso, who came and placed his hand very gently upon the wound on my head. It is our custom, when one wounds another and admits his guilt, for the one inflicting the injury to place his hand upon the wound, so that the injured person obtains relief.

I asked Nyaniso to explain the reason for his sudden attack upon me. He said he would not speak until I had forgiven him. This I did freely. He said: 'Xesibe man, do you not know that our people are of the house of Mayaba and so of royal blood? Our men have ever been famed for holding their own, be it in a battle of wits or a battle of spears, so our women have had something about them raising them above the weaknesses of common women. I do not say it is their bearing or their breeding, but I do say our women are like that and it seemed to me that you, Xesibe man, had either overlooked or forgotten this when you made remarks to me in regard to my sister's relations with that gxagxa (common fellow), Ntuku.' I was glad to hear Nyaniso refer to Ntuku as gxagxa.

I answered: 'But she did not spurn him, she did not reject him; she seemed to find pleasure in his company.' Then it was that Nyaniso gave me a blow harder than the one he had given me with his induku; he said: 'You seem to have interested yourself in the affairs of our family; have you been asked to do so? It seems to me that this day you have brought about a division between your house and my own. We are Mayabas! My father is now grown old and I speak for him. Let your house go about its affairs; we Mayabas are able to look after our own.'

Now my people were of a royal house senior to that of Mayaba; we claimed descent from Ntswaelana. It was our people who maintained our tribal entity at the time when strong clans were being broken up and dispersed by a great power to our eastward. Nyaniso either did not know of or disregarded these things. It was not for me at this stage to remind him of them.

For a long time there was silence between us. Then I said: 'My brother, there is no place for misunderstanding between us. Each of us has been hasty in what we have said and done. There must be no division between our houses; such a thing would bring grief to our parents and unhappiness to ourselves.'

Then we clasped hands, and from that day till the day of his death there was the closest friendship and understanding between Nyaniso and myself.

Nkosi, I have seen many things and my experience has been wide; but when I speak of the death of Nyaniso I speak of what was the greatest sorrow of my life. Pardon me, my chief, if I show a weakness only to be observed in women and children. If you will come on another day I will tell you more.

16

Concerning a Black Horse

Greeting, my Chief! I thank you for the handsome blanket you sent me. It will keep my old bones warm in the winter weather, and I am still able to take pride in its bright colours; it is the envy of the old women. It reminds me of a blanket I bought many years ago after I had dealt successfully with a certain black horse. The horse belonged to a trader named Skwenene (the parrot), who was given that name because to us he somehow looked like a parrot. I used often to go to the store of Skwenene, sometimes to buy, but more often to look at and admire his black horse.

Now we had at our kraal a young horse very much like the horse of Skwenene, the only difference between them being that Skwenene's had a white spot under the saddle and another on the right hind fetlock, whereas ours was altogether black. Then Skwenene's horse being kept at night in a stable and groomed, it was more sleek and shiny than ours.

Skwenene was a poor rider, and it seemed to me that in his hands the horse was, so to speak, wasted. I wished that it were owned by a person who would take real pride and pleasure in it.

I mentioned the matter of this horse to Kwanguba one day, and together we went to the store to see it. He said that our horse was just as good as this one, and if it were properly groomed and fed and at the same time given certain medicines to improve its coat it might look even better. We talked about this, and in the end it was agreed that I should hand our horse over to Kwanguba for two months so that he might see what he could do with it. With the consent of my father he took the horse away.

After two weeks I went over to Kwanguba's place to see our horse. I saw no difference in it except that there was a sore place under the saddle where the hair had come off and there was a similar sore place on the right hind fetlock. I reproached Kwanguba for allowing our horse to be injured. He surprised me by saying that he himself had caused the injuries in the course of his doctoring, but I refrained from saying anything which might displease him, well knowing his powers.

When I was leaving, Kwanguba said I should not see the horse again till the full two months had elapsed, and if I were then dissatisfied with its appearance he would give me two goats, but if I were satisfied I should give him two goats. I agreed to this.

At the end of two months I went to Kwanguba's kraal. For a long time neither of us mentioned the horse. Then I cautiously brought up the subject. Kwanguba appeared to be puzzled, and when I asked him directly to produce our horse he seemed covered with confusion. He said: 'I'm sorry, son of my brother, but your horse is lost. I refrained from reporting the matter at your father's kraal, as I did not wish to rouse your father's displeasure; moreover I expected that the horse might be recovered at any time.'

I reproved Kwanguba, saying that in such a case custom demanded that immediate report should be made to the owner. He replied that no one could be more distressed about the matter than he.

He went out of the hut and told a boy to bring in his horses from the veld. Returning, he said that he would allow me to choose any one of his horses to make up for the loss of ours.

When the troop was brought up, I saw one among them that was black like ours, but its coat was much more sleek and shiny and it had a *white mark* on its right hind fetlock and another under the saddle. I said: 'What is this thing? How do you come to have Skwenene's horse with yours?'

Kwanguba laughed loud and long, then said: 'What sort of a person are you, that you do not recognise your own property? Take your horse, and if you are satisfied give me my two goats; come into the hut and let us talk.'

After he had sworn me to secrecy he told me of all that he had done. He said he knew how much I had admired Skwenene's horse, and thinking that it would please us to make ours as much like that one as possible he had rubbed milk of the Mhlontlo[3] tree on its back and fetlock, which had caused the injuries I had seen, and when the injuries had healed the hair came out white so that our horse had white spots just in the same places and of the same size as Skwenene's. After that he had asked a trader with whom he was friendly to have the horse stabled and groomed, alleging that he was going away from home for a while and that he did not wish it to get into improper hands during that time.

I returned home with the horse and next day sent Kwanguba two goats which he had fairly earned. The same day I rode over to Nyaniso's, partly to show off my beautiful mount before the people of that place, but also to hear what Nyaniso might have to say.

I was pleased that Nyaniso's sister, Nondwe, should be the first at the kraal to see me so finely mounted. This is the girl towards whom Ntuku had made advances and about whom Nyaniso and I had quarrelled and fought. Neither of us had

---

[3] Mhlontlo: euphorbia tree. The sap of this tree is a violent irritant.

referred to her since then, but I had from time to time had a few words with her. She was well called Nondwe (the blue crane). All her movements were stately and there was dignity in her every action. The blue crane is a very beautiful bird.

Nondwe told me that her parents with her brother Nyaniso were at a neighbouring kraal; she would send for them. She called up a kwedini (young boy) to take my horse and invited me to enter her father's hut. We sat down. I found that speech had departed from me, but in the end I stammeringly enquired as to the news of the place. Nondwe said there was no news there. So we sat silent for a long while. I had hoped that Nondwe would say something in praise of my horse, but she said nothing. It is of course unusual for women to express any opinion regarding cattle or horses, things with which they have no dealings, but I thought that my horse would provoke some expression of admiration.

I asked Nondwe at last if she knew that her brother and I were great friends. She said: 'If you are great friends, why do you fight with each other?' Now how was I to reply to this question? I could not tell Nondwe that we had fought on her account, so I replied weakly that we didn't fight, we had merely played with sticks. She smiled at this, and said: 'Play with sticks, so that one of you is almost killed?' I was tempted to tell her the whole truth of my quarrel with Nyaniso, but as that matter had long been dead and buried I decided not to dig it up, and replied that young men *did* occasionally have their foolish moments. She was inclined to pursue the subject, but just then to my relief Nyaniso entered the hut. It seemed to me that his greeting was more effusive than usual. I was pleased at this, and glad that as Nondwe went out of the hut she heard what he said.

I told Nyaniso about the black horse, and we there and then made a plan. We decided that Skwenene's horse should be sold to a man in a distant place whom I knew to be a good rider and fond of horses. As this man knew me, it was not suitable that I should sell the horse to him, and Nyaniso undertook this business.

On a day arranged between us I rode to the town on our black horse and obtained a pass to travel with it in a direction opposite to that which Nyaniso would take with Skwenene's horse. I was careful that the police should see our horse and note its marks. That same evening Nyaniso and I went to Skwenene's place. When it was late and the lights in the house had disappeared, Nyaniso approached the stable, while I kept watch nearer the house to see that we were not observed. Nyaniso entered the stable and brought out the horse. It was as like ours as two mealie grains are alike. Silently we went off into the darkness. When we were some distance away from the store we halted. There, bidding each other farewell and good fortune, we parted. I returned to my home and Nyaniso went away with Skwenene's horse.

Very early next morning I set out for the place mentioned in my pass as my destination. I called in at many kraals on the way and at each unobtrusively drew attention to my horse. I remained a day at the kraal I had arranged to visit, and then returned home.

It was some days later that Nyaniso came to our place. Our meeting and greeting were without words. It is like this in certain circumstances between friends; silence often expresses more than many words.

We sat in the dusk of the hut and lit our pipes. No questions were asked, no information was volunteered. Then Nyaniso, taking several long puffs from his pipe, undid his arm-purse. He shook out from it on to the smeared floor many golden pounds; he spread them out so that I was able to see that they were twenty-five. I knew then that good fortune had attended him on his journey. For a while he left the coins on the floor where they shone in the firelight, then he returned each to its resting-place in his arm-purse.

'Come and see me tomorrow and then we will talk,' he said, as he took his leave.

See, Chief, there was such a bond between us that words were not always necessary. We were at times able to convey to each other unspoken thoughts; in certain circumstances we were able to communicate with each other though great distances might intervene. It has been like this with some of our people, but only between those who lived in close communion. This is one of the mysteries concerning which we do not speak. We know that it is so, but how or why it is so we know not – we leave it like that.

The next day I went to the kraal of Nyaniso's people. Nyaniso told me that he had taken Skwenene's horse to the man of whom I had told him, and there, after much bargaining, had sold it for £25. No untoward thing had happened on the journey thither, the greater part of which had been accomplished by night. He had smeared some black substance on the white spots of the horse so that to the casual observer it would appear altogether black without distinctive marks. We handed £10 of the money to Nyaniso's father and £10 to my father. With the remaining £5 Nyaniso and I went to Skwenene's store, where we heard that the black horse had disappeared and that this had been reported to the police. As it was no concern of ours, we paid no particular attention to the matter, but at the same time we listened with all our ears to what people in the shop had to say of it.

After we had been in the store for some time we announced that we each desired to purchase a blanket. We caused Skwenene to bring down from his shelves very many blankets for our inspection. At last we each made our selection, and after much talk Skwenene agreed to let us have the blankets on credit. We had ample money wherewith to pay, but at that particular time we considered that a display of wealth might be unseasonable. This, Chief, is how I come to say that the blanket you have given me reminds me of other days; but the story of Skwenene's horse, as you will realise, is not yet complete.

In those very days two policemen came to our kraal with a paper. They said they had come to arrest me for the theft of Skwenene's horse. With us there is always a time to resist, and then again there is a time to submit. I offered no resistance.

My father spoke pleasantly with the police, offering them beer and other entertainment. They were not inclined to accept his overtures till he undertook to slaughter a goat, and with the slaughtering promised to hand me over at such time as they might require me.

The slaughtering of a thing with us is not merely a killing and eating, it is a celebration and a ceremony so that one who gives an undertaking at such a time will always fulfil his promise. The policemen of course knew this, and it required no great pressing to induce them to stay at our kraal that night.

I sent for Nyaniso. When he came I told him that I had been arrested for the theft of Skwenene's horse, it having been said that I had been seen riding it about the time it had disappeared. Nyaniso was much distressed at hearing this, and proposed then and there to confess the truth to the police and hand himself over to them. I said this was in no way necessary.

The next day I was taken away by the two policemen, who were respectable men with long service and wide experience. I asked them if it was the law that a man should be arrested for riding his own horse. They said they did not know a law like that, but I was charged with riding Skwenene's horse which had very shortly thereafter disappeared. I left the matter there, and we conversed pleasantly enough about other small affairs.

Eventually we reached the village, where I was lodged in jail. I was told that the case would be heard on the fourth day and was asked if I required any witnesses. I said that a man did not require witnesses to show that he had been riding his own horse, but if any witness were necessary to prove my innocence the one who could do that would be Skwenene.

I will not go through all the details of the case. Skwenene described his horse and said that on a certain day it was found to be missing from the stable. When he had finished speaking I was asked if I had any questions to ask him. I replied that I had no question of importance to ask, but I would like to know if the horse of Skwenene were of a kind that could be in two places at once. He replied that it was not such a horse. Many people testified to having seen me riding a horse such as described by Skwenene. To shorten a very long story, in the end it was clearly shown that at the time I had been seen riding a black horse with white spots Skwenene's horse was actually in his stable. Dumezweni, the Magistrate, reproved Skwenene for having accused me falsely, and I was acquitted.

You will know, Chief, who it was that bought Skwenene's horse for £25! As you had the use of the horse for many years, even up to the time it died, it is for you to put the matter right with Skwenene.

Do not be offended with me, Chief. After all Skwenene was a mean fellow and often charged for things in his store a price far above their value; moreover, did we not spend the greater portion of the £25 in his shop?

17

The Finding of a Wife

I am glad to see you today, Chief. I was afraid that the true story of how you came to be possessed of Skwenene's horse might have offended you. This present of tobacco shows that it is not so. If you are still interested in my small affairs, I will go on with my story.

It was in these days following the disposal of the horse that I somehow found myself more frequently at the kraal of Nyaniso's people than theretofore. Nyaniso was not always there, but I often saw Nondwe, and when she was not there I spoke respectfully with her father. It seemed that the old man had some affection for me. As he was in authority at the kraal, I endeavoured to apply that pleasing unction of which my father hold told me. It had to be applied with the utmost discretion, as he was a wily old man. I sometimes met Ntuku at the kraal, and when this happened rage burned within me. How could they tolerate the fellow? His presence made me silent and surly, the more so as Nondwe, always gracious, laughed at his foolish sallies and seemed not averse to his company.

On one of my visits I met Nondwe at the stream near her kraal where she had gone to draw water. As she filled her earthen pot with the dipper I sat down. It seemed to me that she lingered at the filling of her pot. This pleased me. Her back being turned to me, I was the better able to observe the suppleness of her movements. I asked after the health of her parents and of the news of their place.

She halted in her dipping and speaking over her shoulder said that all was well with her people; as for the news, it seemed that very friendly relations had recently been established between Gwabeni and her father. Glancing at me with maidenly coyness, she said it was not for her, a girl, to know what these friendly relations portended, but where parents put their heads together it often indicated that matters concerning their children were being discussed. As Nondwe spoke, she set down her dipper and picked up a handful of dry sand; this she made to spill slowly between her fingers from one hand to the other. I am able to tell you of all these little things, Chief, because they have remained clear in my memory. As one sees the pebbles at the bottom of a clear pool, so after many years I see Nondwe as she appeared to me beside the stream that day.

At last she rose, plucked a handful of leaves; placing them in the pot to keep the water from spilling, she raised the vessel to her head. I had wished to help her with her burden, but whoever saw a man carry a water-pot on his head?

As Nondwe moved off, the *thing* came to me. It was she that I desired for my wife. As for her marrying Gwabeni's people, that should never be. I realised now why it was that Ntuku's overtures had so much incensed me. I marvelled at my own blindness. That day my eyes were opened. I had known Nondwe from her early childhood. A frank friendliness had always existed between us. She was the child of my father's old associates and sister to my companion. Thoughts of marriage had never entered my head. It is often like this in life. A man fails to see the thing that is before his eyes because his mind is not behind his eyes.

It had become clear to me that Nondwe's reference to the friendly relations between Gwabeni and her father meant that overtures of marriage had been made. This marriage should never take place. If need be, I should twala (carry off) Nondwe, which under certain circumstances custom permitted.

When we got to the kraal I enquired for Nyaniso. He happened to be away, so I took my leave. I did not, however, go straight home. I went to where the cattle were grazing. With cautious questions I ascertained from the herdboys that no new cattle had recently been added to the herd. This reassured me, as I then knew that no cattle had been paid by Gwabeni in earnest of the proposed marriage.

When I got home I told my father that I wished to marry at the kraal of Kumbela, father of Nyaniso. He asked how I was to marry without cattle. I asked if he could not help me in the matter. He made no direct reply, but said the thing would have to be talked. I said that I had obtained cattle before and could pay the dowry with cattle obtained in the same way from the same sources. At this he became very angry; he said: 'Do you propose to pay dowry with cattle that are not your own? Is it you who desire to bring your people into disrepute? If questions are asked of your people-in-law as to whence the cattle have come, what will they answer? You will place danger in the kraal of my old friends, and so doing you will replace affection with enmity. Get out from before my face!' I slunk out of my father's hut, chastened and subdued. I saw that I had still much to learn of the observances of my people.

Next day my father sent for my uncle Kamteni and his son Dumiso. When they arrived my father on some trifling pretext sent me to a distant kraal. I was annoyed at this, as I believed he intended to discuss with my relatives the question of my marriage. I hurried in my errand, and when I returned my uncle and his son were still at our kraal. I was very anxious to know what had taken place, but I was told nothing.

As they were taking their leave, I drew Dumiso aside and

questioned him. He said that my father had discussed the matter of my marriage, that proposals were to be made to Kumbela and that he (Dumiso) was to be my go-between. I was very glad to hear this, as I had always liked and trusted my cousin. Word was sent to Kumbela of our intentions, and a few days later Dumiso came to our kraal dressed up in all his finery, announcing that he was on his way to Kumbela's to make love at that place on my behalf.

Dumiso returned late that day looking very subdued. He said that Nondwe would have none of him, and that she had even hinted that Ntuku had found a place in her affections. I there and then ran to fetch my sticks, intending to go and give Ntuku the worst thrashing he had ever had, but Dumiso pacified me by telling me that Kwanguba had a very strong medicine for girls which would put everything right.

We went to Kwanguba, who surprised us by saying, 'You young men have come to consult me about a girl; it is a matter of marriage. The girl is obstinate; you desire a medicine to make her yield.'[4] We said that this was so. He fetched his medicine bag and from it selected a small parcel of roots. He said that Dumiso was to place a portion of the roots in his pipe when he met the girl, and as he smoked he was to blow smoke into her face, so that she should breathe it into her nostrils; he would then see what he would see.

Dumiso went again to the kraal of Nondwe's people. He found Nondwe and her companions sitting beneath some trees; a little distance apart sat Ntuku and his friends. The two parties were exchanging pleasantries of a doubtful nature. As I have said before, well-bred people can speak of certain things without giving offence. Ntuku's conversation caused Dumiso

---

[4] Native doctors make it their business to be well posted in regard to all current gossip.

to spit; what angered him more was the fact that Ntuku and his friends offered him many veiled insults, all of which he received in silence while the girls were inclined to laugh. He took out his pipe and filled it carefully and, unobserved, mixed with the tobacco a small portion of Kwanguba's medicine. He lit his pipe and suddenly going up to Nondwe he blew smoke in her face, at the same moment mentioning my name. She gasped, coughed and then fainted away. Water was thrown in her face, but she lay quite still.

Suddenly she sprang up and began to laugh and cry and wring her hands; nothing would pacify her. Her companions became alarmed. 'Yo! Yo!' they cried. 'She is poselwaed' (under a love spell). 'What shall we do?' The girls helped her to her home. Dumiso went with them. They put her in a hut and did everything possible to soothe her, but she seemed to see and hear nothing; she continued to sob and laugh, and then she began to call my name, 'Ntsukumbini! Ntsukumbini!' Her parents, much disturbed, told Dumiso, who admitted having been the cause of her condition, to put the matter right. He was powerless and suggested that Kwanguba be called in. The old people said that since Nondwe had kept on calling my name, I should be sent for.

I speedily responded to their message and was shown into the hut where Nondwe lay. The older women who were there looked at me with hostility, while they made remarks of an unfriendly nature which, though not addressed to me directly, were intended for my hearing. I took no notice of these women, but went straight up to Nondwe. I spoke to her, but she seemed not to recognise my voice. She continued to sob and laugh and to cry out my name. I placed my hand upon her forehead, and almost at once she became quiet. Sighing deeply, she turned towards me. As she reached out her hands, I grasped them in my own, and she sank down quietly upon her sleeping-mat, where she soon fell into slumber.

The women had meantime quietly withdrawn from the hut, so that I was for the moment left alone with Nondwe. She seemed to me to be even more beautiful in sleep than when awake. I gently unclasped my hands from her grasp and went out of the hut into the sunlight. I was filled with a great joy and my spirit sprang within me. I looked not to the right hand nor to the left as I went on my way. The name of Nondwe rang in my ears. I knew that I was her accepted lover.

Nkosi, I, who now am old, feel the joy of youth when I think of that day.

I must tell you that we black people seldom speak of these things to each other, much less to a white man, but there has been that between us which causes me to open my heart to you.

It is not always that we marry a girl because we love her. It is sometimes merely that a man desires possession and an old man will often marry a young wife so that she may be a help to his other wives who are growing old, but with Nondwe and me – Nkosi, our people have not words to describe such a relationship. I do not know the customs and manners of white people in such matters, and it may be that our ways differ greatly from your ways, but it seems to me that the love of a man for a maid may be the same with your people as it sometimes is with ours.

Nkosi, Nondwe was very beautiful; among all the young girls of our country there was none like her. As I went about the business of our kraal in those days I sang to myself softly, so that none might overhear – I sang of Nondwe, the blue crane, that beautiful bird:

Nondwe;
Ntaka yami,
Kuzo zonke intaka yiyipina enokufana nawe,
Wena ufika ngexeshana ubuye umke,
Nondwe.

Ndindakukubona ndivuye,
Xeshikweni ungekoyo useluhambeni,
Ukungabiko kwako kundenza buhlungu,
Nondwe.

Hlala nam,
Ukuze ubuhle bako bundonwabise,
Hlala nam,
Ukuze ndibone ubundzwakazi bako,
Ntombi ye Nkosi,
Nondwe.

Nondwe!
Bird of mine,
Which of all the birds may be likened to you?
You who come for a season and again depart,[5]
Blue Crane.

When I see you I am joyful,
When you have gone on your journey,
Your absence saddens me,
Blue Crane.

Stay with me,
So that I may rejoice in your beauty,
Stay with me,
So that I may behold your stateliness;
Daughter of a Chief,
Nondwe.

---

[5] The blue crane is a migratory bird.

Nkosi, do not smile at the quavering song of an old man. I could not sing this song to anyone but you who have an understanding mind. Had you heard me at the time I first sang it very many years ago, you would have been enabled to see Nondwe as she was to me at that time, beautiful and stately.

Though I am today what I am, know that my people are able to trace their line back to the dim, distant past through a long line of Chiefs. Though today we are regarded as ordinary people, there is that in our veins which removes us far above the level of the common folk; so is it with the people of Nondwe.

I see that a kwedini is fetching your horse, my Chief. If you must depart, come again on another day and bring comfort to the latter days of an old man who lives only in the past.

18

A Betrothal and a Journey

Bayete! Son of a Chief. Your presence surprises me pleasantly. I did not think that you would find it possible to visit so soon again at my poor place. Let us go and sit in the shade of the cattle-kraal, where we can talk without being disturbed. The voices of my grandchildren are pleasant in my ears and a joy to my old age, but at times quietness is desired, more especially when I am to talk of things of which I have spoken to no man before.

It was not long after I had cured Nondwe of her crying fit that I gathered together all the girls and young men of our neighbourhood so that we might observe the custom of Mabuza. We dressed ourselves in the best of our beads and blankets and set out for Kumbela's place. We ran at a slow pace, so that our girls should not be tired, and we sang and danced all the way. We had brought with us a long staff with a piece of white cloth fastened at its top.

When we arrived at Kumbela's kraal we planted the long staff in a prominent place, so that it and its white cloth might be seen from far around and so that people might know that a girl at that kraal was being courted. It was at the same time a challenge to all other possible suitors. It sometimes happened that a rival with his friends would pull down a Mabuza staff and make off with it, then a fight would be sure to ensue.

After we had planted the staff we withdrew some little

distance from the kraal and waited for the young people of that place to appear. They soon showed themselves and came towards us singing and dancing. Then our girls joined their girls and their young men came and sat with us. As is our custom, ribald pleasantries were exchanged, most of which were aimed at me. This was not to my liking, so I withdrew a little distance. Nondwe came up to me and handed me a little bag beautifully worked with coloured beads. This was in token of her having accepted me.

I will not tell you of our conversation, my Chief; but as for me, to be near to Nondwe was sufficient. We took no notice of the rude jests that were flung at us by the other men and girls.

We remained at that place for quite a long time, then our parties separated, each going its own way. So we observed the custom of Mabuza.

Not long after this my father called Kamteni and Dumiso to our place to talk over the payment to Kumbela of earnest cattle. We sat beside the cattle-kraal and regarded the cattle as they were brought up for our inspection. After much talk my father instructed a herdboy to pick out a certain fine cow, then another was selected and yet another. My father announced that these were to be handed over at the kraal of Kumbela, at which place marriage had been proposed. I selected a young cow and calf, progeny of the heifer my father had given me years before. It was arranged that on a certain day Kamteni, Dumiso and I would take these five cattle to Kumbela. We sent word that we would be there on that day.

When we got to Kumbela's we drove the cattle into the fold, but we were received as utter strangers. A small boy directed us to a hut in which we were to sleep and where food was provided for us. None of the grown-up people at the kraal appeared. In the morning a small boy came saying Kumbela wished to see us. We went to where he was sitting beside the cattle-kraal. We greeted him and sat down. He asked whither were we going and what was the object of our journey. We said we had come to the end of our journey and that we had brought cattle for a girl.

Kumbela asked where was the girl? Kamteni said: 'We wish to marry this kraal of yours.' After this there was silence for a long time; no one spoke.

Then Kumbela said: 'Where are the cattle you speak of and how many are there?' Kamteni got up and brought the cattle to where Kumbela was sitting. We could see that he was pleased with the animals, but he said: 'Do you insult this kraal by proposing marriage with five miserable beasts?'

Kamteni said: 'My Chief, there is starvation at our place and we are poor people. These cattle are the best from our small herd.'

There was much further talk of this nature. In the end Kumbela agreed to accept the five cattle in earnest of the marriage, on condition that we brought one more beast. The marriage would take place when we had paid six further cattle. He received from us the uswazi (the assegai) we had brought with us. This was a token that our offers had been finally accepted and that the bargain was concluded.

Two goats were slaughtered and we remained at the kraal the whole of that day, feasting and drinking beer. It was after the goats had been slaughtered that we were no longer regarded as strangers. That night Nondwe and two other girls shared with us the hut that had been set apart for us. So was my betrothal celebrated.

On my return home my father made it clear that he would not be able to assist me further with dowry cattle, and suggested that it would be as well for me to go out to work and earn money.

I consulted with Nyaniso and Dumiso concerning the question of going to work. We had heard that work with good pay was offering at the gold mines for strong, healthy men.

You see, Nkosi, in those days a gold mine was a new thing to us. We were told that a place had been found where gold could be dug up from the ground. It seemed to me to be a good place, the more so as I was to be paid for digging up the very thing I required. I said we should start off at once, but my father, always cautious, said that we should first consider carefully whether this was not some white man's trick. We had so often been told that a thing was very good and, when we came to test it, it was found to be not very good and sometimes very bad.

After talking over the matter many times from all sides we three young men decided to go and dig up gold. Someone had told us that we were to dig the gold for our masters. Even if that were so it would be a very simple matter to place a piece in one's tobacco-bag from time to time.

You will see, Nkosi, that we knew very little at that time of the gold mines. Nowadays our young men know them well and always go there to earn money. They are even given money before they go to work to induce them to 'join' (contract themselves for labour).

The journey to the mines was long and confusing, but we managed to reach there safely. I said the first thing we must do was to buy spades and dig for ourselves; why should we work for any master and give him the gold. We were still talking about this when a big Zulu man came to us asking if we wanted work. We decided that it might be as well to try what the work was like, and if it was not to our liking we would work for ourselves.

The Zulu man said he knew of a place where there was nice work where he might obtain employment for us. There was much work that was hard and unpleasant which was easy to get, but it was difficult to get nice work. If we each gave him ten shillings, he would take us to a nice master. We demurred to this – why should we pay to get work? The Zulu said that seeing we were strangers he was wishing to do us a kindness, so many people wished to work for this nice master that he had more labourers than he knew what to do with, but he would be able to get us this work by bribing the foremen.

This Zulu man spoke very pleasantly with us and seemed not to care whether we paid him the ten shillings or not. He told us that whether we went with him or not was our own affair, but he had seen so many men who had come to the mines for the first time, who worked very hard, who were paid very little and often were cheated out of their wages.

This man, who said his name was Kumalo, talked to us very pleasantly. He told us a great deal about the mines and about his own country and people. Suddenly he jumped up from the place where we had been sitting and said that we had so much interested him with our conversation that he had almost forgotten that he had to be back at his work at that moment. His master, he said, was a very kind man and might excuse his being a little late, but for that very reason he must hasten so as to be back at the right time.

Excusing himself, Kumalo turned away from us hurriedly and was making off when we stopped him; each of us handed him ten shillings, begging him to secure us employment at the place of which he had spoken. He took the money and shook each of us by the hand in a friendly way, at the same time saying that he could not remain talking with us because he might be late for his work. If we would meet him the next day at the same spot, a little earlier, he would meantime have arranged everything for us.

Nkosi, I am still looking for that man.

The next day we went to the spot arranged at the appointed time. We waited and waited but Kumalo did not appear. We never saw him again.

We were men used to dealing with people like ourselves in our own country. The people of this ugly town at the mines seemed to be of a different kind. Nevertheless, I afterwards realised that my ten shillings was not wasted. The spending of it enabled me to avoid many traps of a similar kind.

If I saw Kumalo today I would ask him to drink beer with me. Though he took money from men who were strangers in a strange place, men who then were glad to be spoken to in a friendly manner, yet he did good to us and we three afterwards laughed over the matter and thanked Kumalo for the lesson he had taught us. So I say that I am still looking for Kumalo. For him I would slaughter a fat goat and I would place a brimming beer-pot between his knees.

Must you go, Chief? I know that my laughter is now like the cackling of an old hen. It is not often that I laugh, but when I think of Kumalo there is that which moves me to mirth. Nkosi, that man stabbed us with our own assegai.

I will hold your stirrup, my Chief, while you mount. The horse you are riding is not nearly so fine a one as the black one with white spots that you bought from Skwenene.

My Chief, go pleasantly and with safety.

19

At the Mines

When last you came to my place, Chief, laughter filled me, as I held your stirrup.

It is like that: one day is full of sunshine, another has scattered clouds, a third is cold and bleak.

Kwowu! Chief, those first days at the mines were terrible – fearsome.

As I have said, we waited for the man who said his name was Kumalo. I had known that Kumalo was a name for good reasons honoured among the Amazulu. This fellow who came to us at a time when we desired a friend was not really of the Kumalo clan, but knowing that this was an honoured name he made use of it to our discomfiture for the time being, but also to our advantage in the end. After our experience with this man we were wary. Several people came to us offering to make things easy; others said they would take us to places where brandy was to be had in plenty; some said if we went with them we would find delights that we had never heard of; but by that time we were awake to the dangers that lay behind the friendly overtures of strangers.

So we endured several unpleasant days till we encountered a man who told us what we knew to be the truth of things. He told us that the work we would have to do would be hard, that much would have to be endured; but if we worked well, in the end good money would be placed in our hands.

We went with that man, who took us to several strange places where we were questioned and looked at by certain white men who seemed to be tired of looking at black people. In the end we were taken to a place of high walls. There were many dwellings within this place and very many men lived there together. There were white men who seemed to be in authority and spoke harshly to all who did not immediately obey their orders. My mind becomes confused when I think of those days – all seemed confusion; it may not have been so, but to us it appeared that there was no reason or order in anything, so much so that I find it hard to tell you of all we underwent at the time. This was very long ago and the young men who go to the gold mines in these days tell me that things are very different. Though the work is hard, there is much done by the white masters to make life less unpleasant.

I cannot tell you, Chief, of all that befell us in those days, but the memory of the first day that I entered the bowels of the earth is not a memory; it is like an evil dream from which one wakes with a shudder.

We are a people who love the open spaces, the long distances, the sunlight and the freedom which our country gives us.

We, with a number of other men, were taken to a certain place where there was a high structure of wood. Great trees must have been felled to provide the timber from which this structure was created. At the top was a wheel which spun round; below was a small house near which we were instructed to assemble. We went to that place, and at an order we entered a box made of iron; many went into that box.

Suddenly the box began to descend. I felt as if my bowels were leaving me, a sickness overcame me, there was a roaring in my ears. As we went down life and sunlight were left behind.

After what seemed to me a very long time the iron box stopped and we got out. We found ourselves in a long cave. The air was stifling. The place was filled with crashing, clanging noises; small lights flitted about, some near, some distant. These were the little lamps carried by the workers. I was bewildered by all these sights and sounds, but was brought to my senses by a sharp order from a white man who told us to take our tools and follow him. We had each been given an iron bar, sharp at one end, a heavy hammer and a little lamp.

We followed the white man along the cave to its end; then we were told to make holes in the solid rock with our iron bars and hammers. I saw that other men were already at that work. I was watching to see and learn how the holes were to be made when I received a sudden stinging blow on my cheek which felled me to the ground. As I picked myself up I saw the white man standing over me, threatening me with a large iron bar. He cursed me for a lazy pig and ordered me to get on with my work at once. As in a dream I picked up my drill and hammer and tried to do with them what I saw other men doing. After a while I found that the work was not so difficult as it had at first appeared. I smote my drill with my hammer, making myself think that each blow was falling upon the head of the white man who had struck me.

So we worked on hour after hour. Sweat poured from me, my muscles were like to crack; but I dared not stop, as I felt that the eyes of the white man were upon me.

This, then, was the way gold was won! It is not surprising that it is so highly prized, being earned by the sweat and blood of men.

When we were told to cease work, I took my little lamp and searched round about for pieces of gold, but I found none, nor did I ever find any all the time I worked at that place.

I will not tell you, Nkosi, of each day's work; one was

117

much like another. As a man may accustom himself to almost anything, so I got used to the making of holes. It was comforting to feel that Nyaniso and Dumiso were working close beside me and to know there was sunshine outside that dark hole.

All the time I worked I pondered in my mind how I might be revenged upon the white man who had struck me. I had seen him strike and even kick other men, and one day he smote a man with an iron bar so that he broke the man's arm. There was some inquiry into this, but the white man explained that a rock had fallen, causing the injury. There the matter ended.

I must now tell you, Chief, of the last day I worked at that place.

We went down as usual in the iron box and began work at our appointed places. Nyaniso and I were close to each other; Dumiso was some little distance from us. Almost the only sound at the moment was the click, click, of many hammers striking upon many drills. The white man of whom I have spoken was near to us.

Suddenly there was a roaring, rending, splitting crash; then darkness and comparative silence. It took me some moments to collect my senses and to realise that a great mass of rock with smaller fragments had fallen from above us. I could not believe that, but for a few cuts, I was uninjured. What woke me to reality was a feeble call from the darkness near at hand. I groped about and at last found my overturned lamp, which I managed to light. I made my way over the piles of fallen rock to where I had heard the cry for help.

Nkosi, even today my heart turns to water when I think of what I saw. There was Nyaniso lying with a heavy piece of rock upon his shoulder and chest. He could not move. He called to me with a feeble voice: 'Oh my brother, come to me. I have been killed in this terrible place. I shall no more look upon the sunlight.' I moved the rock which had crushed him, but I could see that he was dying before my eyes. Blood streamed from his many wounds. He kept on saying, 'I have been killed in this terrible place; I have been killed in this terrible place.' What could I do? There he lay dying before my eyes.

I held his hands and spoke such words of comfort as arose to my mind. His voice grew more feeble. He asked me to bend down closer so that he might feel I was near him. He opened his eyes and looked into mine. I could see that his spirit was about to take its flight. His last words were: 'As you have been a brother to me, so you will be a son and a comfort to my parents – farewell.' A gasping, shuddering sigh and he was no more.

Oh, Nkosi, as I sat there I buried my face in my arms and wept. I had sat I know not how long when it seemed to me I heard a groan of pain. I picked up my lamp and went towards the sound. There I saw the white man who had struck me. Across his legs lay a large piece of rock. His body writhed with pain. For a moment I was glad to see this. It seemed to me that this white man was the author of the evil that had befallen us. Unreasoning rage consumed me.

I picked up a heavy bar of iron and approached him. 'Ha, white man,' I said, 'this is the last day of your evil life.' I lifted the iron bar to strike.

At that moment his eyes met mine. He did not flinch, but his eyes were like those of a stricken buck under the spear of a hunter. Reason returned to me; the iron bar dropped from my hands.

Nkosi, I was saved from a horrible thing – I was about to smite a stricken, helpless man!

With that very iron bar I was able to remove the rock that lay across the white man's legs. I moved him to a more comfortable place. I found a shirt he had discarded, and with it did my best to bind up his wounds.

119

All these things happened in quite a short space of time. I had not been able to think clearly. After I had made the white man as comfortable as I could, the thought came to me: why had no one come to our aid? I picked up my lamp and made my way in the direction from which we had come to work. I had not gone far when I found that the whole passage was blocked by masses of fallen rock. I shouted and shouted. The only response was the dull echo of my own voice.

I returned to the white man and told him what I had found, but his pain seemed too great for him to realise the fearfulness of our position. He cried out for water. I brought him water, which he drank greedily. This seemed to give him some relief. As I sat beside him my eyes fell upon the iron bar with which I would have struck him. Shame burned within me. I could not take my eyes from that iron bar, so I decided to put it in a place where I could not see it. As I was removing it I remembered that with it I had removed the rock which had fallen on the white man. Then the thought came to me that where I had moved one rock I might move many. I looked at the iron bar as I held it in my hands. A little spark of hope sprang up in my heart. It was then that I remembered Nyaniso's last words: 'As you have been a brother to me, so you will be a son and a comfort to my parents.'

Courage, strength, hope came to me. I fell upon the mass of loose rock with the iron bar. I pushed and pulled and levered. I worked like a mad person. I would somehow open a way of escape. I worked on desperately, madly. Then I heard the white man calling. I went to him and found he was quite out of his senses. He talked of many things. Much of what he said I could not understand, but I gathered that he had a brother named Jim with whom he had quarrelled and with whom he wished to make his peace before he died. It seemed that this quarrel had embittered the whole of his life, and had caused

120

him to sink down far below the level of his people, who were Chiefs in their own country. So it had come about that instead of associating with people of his own class he had become a 'shift boss' in this mine.

His rambling speech was difficult to follow and some of it was a mere mumbling. At last he became silent and fell into a fitful sleep, so I returned to my work. I tried to keep my mind, as I struggled and strove, upon what I was doing, so that I should not think of other things that pressed heavily upon me. I worked till my hands were bleeding and torn, my body and feet were cut by the sharp points of broken rock. It seemed that I made little progress, but I must go on. Then a piece of rock I had dislodged fell upon my foot and crushed it.

I limped back to where the white man lay. He had waked from his troubled sleep and was now in his sound senses. He called me to him and asked what I had been doing. When I had told him he said: 'You may be a damned black nigger, but you are white right through.'

Nkosi, it took me a long time to understand what these words meant, and as I returned to my work of moving rock I turned them over in my mind and committed them to memory. It seemed to me to be a good speech.

I worked till I was utterly exhausted, my crushed foot was causing me the greatest pain, so I went and sat down and rested beside the white man, who was very weak from loss of blood. He wished to speak and I did not hinder him. 'Black nigger,' he said, 'I do not know your name, nor do I know or care whence you have come; that does not matter now, nothing matters very much. We are in our graves. This fall of rock is such that by the time it is removed I will be dead. You may or may not see the sunlight again. If you do win back to life, you will go to my brother who lives at a place of which I will tell you. It may be hard to find that place, but you must keep on asking for it till you find it. Then you will tell my brother of all that has befallen us here, not omitting to mention the manner in which you have helped me. You will give my brother this small package, which will explain much to him, and it may be that he will forgive me and at the same time accept forgiveness from one whom he thinks has done him great wrong.'

When this man had finished speaking, he lay back regarding me closely. I cared not to meet his gaze, so I cast my eyes in another direction.

I said: 'White man, today you and I have received many wounds. The wounds from which you suffer are in your body, while mine are not only in my body, but also in my very soul. One who has through life been closer to me than a brother has been taken from me. That is a matter of which I will not speak further. Your bodily wounds and mine are the same in that they cause us to feel pain and that blood flows from them. One man may not see the inward hurt that another suffers, yet the pain is there.

'You are a white man; my skin is black, yet there is no difference in the colour of the blood we have shed this day. So, white man, if ever again I see the sunlight, your brother will be found and your message delivered. There is that within me which says that we both shall come through this thing – hope on, while I work.'

I returned to the moving of rocks but, Nkosi, I had now been some two days as far as I could judge without food and my strength was giving out. It was the last words of Nyaniso that gave me strength to keep on.

It was while I was struggling to move a very big rock that a booming sounded in my ears, rushing waters seemed to cover me and I knew no more.

When I began to come to my senses the first thing I saw was a very small light moving about in the distance. This light grew bigger and bigger till my eyes could no longer bear it. Then I heard voices – people were passing. Away in the distant dim lights I saw people bending over something, then I saw them carrying something very carefully coming towards me. As they got to near where I was lying they put their burden down. Then I heard the faint voice of the white man who had been with me. He said: 'There's a nigger somewhere about here; look for him, he's badly hurt, and he has stood by me.' A voice replied: 'I've seen him; he is dead; never mind him.' I cannot repeat the exact words of the conversation, but this is as near as I can remember it. I lay perfectly still. No one seemed to notice me, though by now many people were passing. One thing repeated itself in my mind: 'He is dead; never mind him.'

I saw men carry away the body of Nyaniso, and I saw that he was being carried silently and even carefully. As the men passed I whispered, 'Rest in peace, my brother.' All this while I lay perfectly still; indeed, I do not think I could have moved had I wished to do so; though my mind was alive, my body was dead.

After a long while I saw a party of men preparing to ascend by way of the iron box. Stealthily I crept towards them and in the dim light mingled with them unnoticed. The words, 'Never mind him; he is dead', kept repeating themselves in my mind. People thought I was dead. I would leave them to think this. Nyaniso was so very like me in appearance that he would be easily mistaken for me.

We ascended in the iron box. No one seemed to take notice of me. When we got to the top I got out of the box to find that it was night. I slipped away into a dark shadow, waiting and listening. I heard snatches of talk: 'The white man is alive; he was helped by Ntsukumbini – Ntsukumbini is dead, but where is the third man who was shut up with them? The white people all say that their friend would never have been found alive had it not been for Ntsukumbini.' This and much more I heard while I hid in the dark shadow.

Then I saw Dumiso passing. I went out to him and grasped him by the arm, making at the same time a sign that he should be silent. I whispered to him the facts of what had occurred and begged him to get my things together, placing with them some food. This place, I said, would see me no more.

With Dumiso's aid I was able to make my escape, which was no easy matter. When daylight came I was very far from that cursed place where men are killed as they work for those who receive the gold at the price of men's lives.

As the sun rose I found myself near a wooded stream. Here I washed the dried blood from my many wounds. Then I lay in the sunlight, thinking joyfully that I would be out in the sunshine all that day and all of the next. I partook of some of the food Dumiso had provided for me as I lay basking and resting.

I did not move off from that place till late in the afternoon when the shadows were long. While it was light I kept along the wooded course of the river. When night came I made off into open country and westward in which I believed to be the direction of my home, just as in springtime a horse will stray towards the place where he was foaled.

So several days passed. The food that Dumiso had obtained for me had not lasted me long in my famished state. I must now either beg or die of hunger and exhaustion.

It was late afternoon on the fifth day that I made for a homestead, all of which I had so far carefully avoided. I found this to be a farmhouse, so I sought out the place where the farm workers lived. The labourers received me with surprise, asking whether I did not know that this was the place of Baas Rooi Piet, who dealt very harshly with wanderers. I said I cared not for the name of their master; all I desired was a little food and a great deal of rest.

These people gave me food and a place to sleep on condition that I left there very early in the morning, making it appear as if I had only just arrived at that place. I agreed to this, being entirely exhausted and famished with hunger.

Before dawn I gathered my things together and went away into the veld. I came back to the farmhouse just as the sun was rising. As I approached the house I saw a very big white man with a red beard and red hair. I knew this must be Rooi Piet.

I went up to him respectfully and asked if he could give me work. He looked me up and down and asked what kind of work I was able to do. I said, thinking quickly, that I was able to work with sheep, but that I would do my best at any work he might have to offer me.

Again Rooi Piet looked me up and down and then he smiled. Nkosi, I call it a smile because he was a white man, but to me it was the smile of a vicious dog when baring his teeth to bite.

He asked me from whence I had come and where I had worked before. I told him the true story of how and why I had escaped from the mines.

Again he bared his teeth. 'Ho ho!' he said. 'So you have run away from the mines, have you? If I hand you over to the police, you will be kept in jail for a very long time and you will also be made to finish your time in the mines.'

I begged him not to tell the police. The thought of returning to the mines was too fearful.

In the end he agreed to give me work, but said that if I misbehaved myself in any way he would hand me over to the police. So I took service with Baas Rooi Piet.

I did my best to keep out of my master's way, as he appeared to me to be a bad man. I had seen him thrash a young boy with a sjambok for some slight mistake the boy had made and I was afraid that a similar thing might happen to me. I was always afraid, too, that I might be given over to the police, so I worked well and hard. I had thoughts of leaving the place secretly and making my way home, but I could not go home without money.

You see, Nkosi, the thought of Nondwe had all this time been in my mind. I had set out to earn money, so that I should be able to buy the six cattle still required before I could marry her.

Yes, my Chief, it is getting late and you have far to go, so I will not detain you, but come again when you can spare the time to sit and talk with a poor old man whose life is all behind him. Hamba kahle Nkosi.

20

At the Farms of Rooi Piet and Baas Jim

Welcome, Chief, come inside; it is cold and bleak without and the wind is bitter. The children will make up the fire for you and roast some amaqobo (cobs of maize) of which I know you are fond. I see that rain is threatening; maybe you will find it possible to stay the night with us. The guest hut is fresh and clean. This would not be for you the first night spent at a Xesibe kraal. The Silangwes tell me that you have often been to their place on top of the mountains while on your hunting expeditions and that you have stayed with them, partaking of such food and lodging as they were able to provide. Those people also tell me that it is there you were given your name – 'Mpondozeliza', horns of the rhebuck. They say that in a time of starvation you shot a rhebuck and gave all the meat to the children, so that for one night they went to rest with full bellies.

This reminds me, Chief, of old Ndumndum, who was a personage in the Silangwe clan. He was, as you know, a policeman. Even after he left the police and received a pension at the hands of Government, still he kept a sharp lookout for those whom he considered to be wrongdoers – but I am finishing this story before I have begun it.

I was telling you of my work at the farm of Baas Rooi Piet. I worked well at that place for a month and at the end of that month I asked Rooi Piet to pay me my wages. He said: 'Your wages are that I do not hand you over to the police; be satisfied with that.'

Nkosi, I was afraid of his words and I worked on, saying nothing.

Baas Rooi Piet was a breeder of horses and that fact was the one thing that kept me at his place. I have ever loved a good horse, as you know, my Chief, and I speak without offence; the black horse with white spots that I selected for you was a good horse.

The horses of Rooi Piet were kept on a distant part of the farm, and though their care was not a part of my work I often found time to go to where they were. As you may know, there is a particular kind of whistle that horses like. It is the same as one uses when milking a young cow unused to the hands of men. When one whistles like this, the cow stands quiet and yields her milk freely. So with the horses; when I whistled in this particular way they allowed me to approach them and handle them, though by other people on the farm they were regarded as wild things.

It was after one of my visits to the horses that I came upon Baas Rooi Piet near his homestead. He was in a great rage. He was shouting at one of his shepherds, accusing him of having stolen three sheep which had been missed. The shepherd, cowering before Rooi Piet's wrath, said he knew nothing of the loss of the sheep; they had disappeared in the night and jackals must have taken them.

Rooi Piet dashed off into his house and reappeared carrying a sjambok in one hand and a gun in the other. He ordered the remaining servants to lay hold upon the herd and take him to a shed nearby. They dared not disobey. The unfortunate herd was tied by the wrists, the end of the cord was passed over a beam and pulled so that the tips of his toes just touched the ground. Rooi Piet was in a frenzy of rage. He tore off his coat

128

and bared his arms. He said: 'This herd says there are jackals on this farm. This is how I deal with jackals of this kind.' He thrashed that boy till the blood flowed. He kept on thrashing till he was out of breath. The boy had fainted and hung by his wrists like a dead person. He had kept on crying out till he was able to speak no more: 'The jackals have taken them; the jackals have taken them.'

Suddenly Rooi Piet's glance fell upon me. He ordered the servants to tie me up and, to strengthen his orders, he picked up his gun. I offered no resistance as I felt no guilt, and the people who laid their hands upon me then had, when I first came, received me kindly at great risk to themselves.

I was taken and tied to a waggon wheel by my wrists and ankles. Rooi Piet shouted at me. He said he'd seen me skulking about in distant parts of the farm; I had not helped to tie up the herdboy and he knew that for this and other reasons I was joint with the herd in the theft of the sheep.

He took a deep breath and laid his sjambok across my bare shoulders. Nkosi, the agony of it. The first blow was like the burning of a hot iron. My body writhed with pain, I could not control it, but I uttered no sound. This seemed to enrage Rooi Piet, for he redoubled his blows. I could feel the warm blood trickling down my back.

At last Rooi Piet's anger seemed to have spent itself. He strode away muttering to himself, and at that moment my senses left me.

When I regained consciousness I saw standing beside me a little white boy. The child regarded me with wide, staring eyes. I was still tied to the waggon wheel.

I saw that the eyes of the child were full of tears. He spoke very softly to me, saying, 'Poor black thing, poor black thing. Why did you enrage my father?' He took a knife from his pocket and cut my bonds. I staggered to a neighbouring stone, where I sat down. The child continued to speak in a kind way: 'Poor black thing, go now to your hut and I will send old Hottentot Koos to you. He knows all about Hottentot medicines and he will give you something which will soon ease your pain and heal your wounded back.'

This lad told me that his father sometimes went to the village, where he drank much brandy, and on his return he was like a wild creature. He had even then gone to the village and might not be back for some days; I had better run away before he returned.

Just then a voice called from the house and the little boy ran away.

I dragged myself to my hut and lay down. The burning of my back was as if there were a fire of coals upon it.

Later on old Hottentot Koos came to me. He was a very ugly little old man, but his hands were gentle as he poured upon my back and rubbed in the medicine he had brought. All the time he doctored me he sang softly in a strange language. It seemed that, with his song, he was helping the medicine to do its healing work.

I remembered the boy who had been flogged in the shed and asked Koos to go to him. He soon returned, saying the boy was beyond the need of medicine – the boy was dead.

Old Koos sat down in my hut. He took some roots from his bag; these he threw on the fire. The smoke from the roots gave a pleasant scent, and as the smoke rose Koos began to sing, while he swayed his body from side to side. I could not make out the words of the song, I do not know if there were words, but it was like the crooning of a mother to her babe. It was also like a wail of mourning.

I watched this strange little man for quite a long time till my eyelids grew heavy; then I dropped off into a deep sleep.

When I woke I found it was daylight and Koos had gone.

The pain of my stripes was not so great as I had expected. I thought to myself that this strange little Hottentot was a great doctor, even greater than Kwanguba. As I lay thinking, Koos entered the hut. He was very ugly; he was short in stature, wrinkled, and he looked very much like a monkey – especially his eyes, which were light brown and alert – darting this way and that as those of a monkey.

Koos sat down in silence while he groped in his bag, from which he took a number of bones; these he threw up in the air, and when they fell on the floor he observed the position in which they lay. He threw them up again and again, each time closely regarding the position in which they lay.

All the while he sang in a soft, crooning way. Then he gathered the bones together and replaced them in his bag.

For the first time he regarded me directly and began to speak. 'There are many things you desire to know, and I may be able to tell you of some of these things.

'The carcasses of the missing sheep you will find in a certain kloof on the mountainside where they have been killed and partly eaten by jackals.[6]

'After you leave this place you will find a man whom you seek.

'There is a young girl who lives at a distant place – she bears you in mind. I can tell you nothing further.'

It was this last saying of old Koos that stirred me into life – Nondwe was bearing me in her mind. I questioned the old man and kept on questioning him, but his only answer was: 'I

---

[6] There is nothing very remarkable in the doing of old Koos. He had no doubt come upon the carcasses of the sheep; it was quite likely that a young man like Ntsukumbini should have a girl waiting for him, and old Koos had probably gone through Ntsukumbini's belongings while he slept and seen the package addressed to Jim. At the same time Hottentot diviners have been known to do extraordinary and unexplainable things with the throwing of bones.

can tell you nothing further – be satisfied.'

I got up and dressed myself – Koos crept out of the hut. I did not see this strange little man again till many years had passed.

As I was about to leave the hut the little white boy who had come to me the day before and cut my bonds appeared at the door. 'Poor black thing,' he said. 'I know that Koos will have done you much good with his medicines; wait here till the maid brings you a cup of good hot coffee.'

The boy was darting away, but I stayed him. I took his little white hand in mine. As one does to a Chief, I kissed the back of his hand signifying that I was under his protection, and I kissed the little pink palm of it showing my appreciation of his kindness and his bounty. The little boy snatched his hand from mine and ran away. As he went he rubbed his hand on his clothes, as if to wipe out the unseen mark I had desired to leave on it. Who knows that but my mark may still be there, seen only with the eyes of a little white boy who had acted kindly towards a stricken black man.

The maid brought me a steaming beaker of coffee and, placing it on the floor of my hut, she withdrew. I looked at the beaker and I looked up at the house. There I saw the little white boy. I raised my hand to him and gave him the salute that one gives to Chiefs – Bayete! The boy waved his hand and disappeared within the house.

Knowing that Baas Rooi Piet was away and would be unlikely to return for some time, I took my ease that day. I made a pretence of work, and in the afternoon I went up to the kloof on the mountainside that had been indicated by old Koos. There I saw the mangled, rotting carcasses of the three missing sheep for the loss of which the life of a lad had been taken. Some day Rooi Piet would pay for this, as he would pay for the stripes upon my back.

When I got back to my hut the sun was setting. I made up the fire and as it spread its light I saw there was a package among my things which I had not seen before. I examined this and found it to contain food. On the paper wrapper was written the one word 'Go'. This could only have been written by the little white boy and I knew that I must act upon his direction. I hid the package of food in the hut and then went to where the other farm workers lived. They were gathered together in one hut round a smouldering fire. There was silence among them – they were mourning. The young lad who had died under the lash was of their people. I did not understand the way of these folk, their spirit seemed to be broken. For years they had worked on the farm of Rooi Piet – kicks, blows and thrashings had been their daily portion; these were part of the life to which they had become used. They would like to escape from it, but whither would they go? They had no country they could call their own. There they stayed on, not knowing what a day might bring forth.

Their talk was despondent and depressing. I asked, was there not a little white boy on the place? At this question life seemed to spring into their dull faces. They said this little boy, son of Rooi Piet, was as a ray of sunshine on a dark day. He had prevented many thrashings by pleading with his father for those accused of wrongdoing. He had even interposed his small body between his father's lash and a bare back, so that Rooi Piet had stayed his hand in act to smite. Whatever Rooi Piet's faults might be, he was as clay in the hands of this child.

All that these people said was good hearing to me who had been befriended by the small boy, and I was glad to know from them that his kindness to me was not mere caprice. I bade these people good night and returned to my own place. I sat long by the dying fire till the chill of dawn aroused me from my half-dreaming thoughts.

I had made up my mind to leave the farm, to take the risk of being caught, flogged and then perhaps handed over to the police as a deserter from the gold mines. I had been paid no wages for the time I had worked, but I had a plan for the adjustment of that matter – then there was my flogging; nothing could put that right, nothing remove the scars from my back, but I would find an ointment, and that ointment would come from the farm of Baas Rooi Piet.

I gathered my things together and as I arranged them I came upon a small round looking-glass with a metal cover that I had bought at the mines. This I would leave for the little white master who had befriended me. I wrapped it in the piece of paper on which was written the word 'Go', and I placed the package in a prominent place on the stoep of the house. The package would be found and the child would know from whom the contents had come.

As I left that place I saluted that little boy as Chiefs are saluted – Bayete! In his warm bed he would know nothing of this, yet again I raised my arm and saluted – Bayete! Then I made off westward as the dawn began to show pink – pink like the palm of the small hand I had kissed in gratitude.

Nkosi, as I left that place it seemed to me that I had cast away a heavy burden; at the same time I carried in my breast the memory of a small white child who had shown me kindness.

I strode off into the fresh air of early morning and then I broke into a swinging run. I hoped that Rooi Piet would drink much brandy and keep drinking, so that he would not discover my absence too soon.

As I ran on in the early morning I sang, and it was the song of the blue crane that I sang – Nondwe!

Now while I was at Rooi Piet's I had made enquiries as to

the whereabouts of the place that had been described to me by the brother of Jim. Some said this, some said that, and in the end I concluded it was somewhere towards the westward, so I kept on towards the west. I felt also that in that direction lay my own home. When I came to villages I avoided them; when I came to homesteads in the country I passed them by. So I went on for five days.

I had used the food given me by Rooi Piet's little son very carefully, but it had given out and I found that hunger was taking away from my feet that swinging stride that had been theirs. I walked where before I had run and the walking was slow and painful, the more so as I was hungry; but I kept on. Then on a day I sank down at the roadside. I could go no further. My spirit melted within me. I was overcome by great weakness and weariness. I fell into what was like deep slumber, but it was not sleep; my mind and body just refused to do their work.

I do not know how long I had lain in this state when I was aroused by the barking of a dog quite close to me. I saw that it was a white man's dog of the kind we call ibaku (pointer), then I saw a man on horseback approaching. The man carried a gun. For the instant I thought he was Rooi Piet and was about to dash off, when the man called to me. I saw then that it was not Rooi Piet. He asked what I was doing there lying drunk by the roadside. I said I was not drunk, I was dead with weariness and hunger. He regarded me closely for a moment, then told me to follow him.

We went some distance and passing round a bend in the path we came upon a homestead which had been out of sight behind a hill.

The man called to a servant to take his horse and at the same time told the servant to give me food and a place to sleep.

The servant took me to the huts where the labourers lived

and gave me food – amasi (sour milk) and stamped mealies. I thought I had never before tasted such delicious food.

As the food began to do its nourishing work, my mind cleared and thoughts came to me – this white man who had found me seemed to be kind. I would ask him to give me work. As I was thinking about the white man it seemed to me that I had seen him somewhere before. This puzzled me. Memory is a strange thing; it sometimes refuses to be captured, like an unruly calf that refuses to be driven into the kraal.

I slept that night like one dead and woke in the morning greatly refreshed. As I lay in my sleeping-place a servant came to say that Baas Jim wished to see me.

Baas Jim! Memory came rushing upon me. This must be the brother of the white man with whom I had been in the mine, this was why his face was familiar to me.

He questioned me closely – whence had I come, where had I worked before, how came I to be lying starving by the roadside?

I replied in this way: 'Nkosi, my story is a long one, part of it is written upon my back in words of blood.' At the same time I bared my back.

Baas Jim gave a long whistle as he regarded my back, then he said: 'What did you do to deserve such a terrible thrashing?'

I replied: 'Nkosi, I was accused of having stolen three sheep.'

At that Baas Jim sprang up. He said I had received all that I deserved; he wanted no stealers of sheep on his farm, and he angrily bade me be gone.

I said: 'Nkosi, you have not yet heard my story. I have suffered much; the tale of my suffering would take a long time. Those three sheep I never stole. I may have done much that in the eyes of the white people is wrong, but those sheep I did not steal.'

Baas Jim sat down, regarding me with suspicion. I met his gaze firmly.

'If you tell me a parcel of lies,' he said, 'I will see that the stripes on your back are doubled; get on with your story.'

Now, Nkosi, I had that with me which I felt might secure the goodwill of this stern man, but the time seemed unseasonable for me to place before him a certain small package; moreover, I did not wish that package to be a source of gain to myself; the circumstances under which I had undertaken to deliver it were such that I could not bring myself to use it to my own advantage.

I told Baas Jim in a few words the story of how I had worked at Rooi Piet's farm, of the death of the herdboy under the lash, of my own flogging and of my escape; but I mentioned nothing of the mines, that was a matter which could wait.

In the end Baas Jim said he believed my story and undertook to give me work, which would be the care of his horses. I had told him I knew something of horses and their ways.

I worked at that place pleasantly enough. I found that Baas Jim was a stern but just man. When with much trouble I had mastered a particularly unruly young horse, he added something to my wages. Each coin I received I hid carefully in the thatch of my hut. I would soon have enough money to buy a cow. I would work on till I had the wherewithal to buy six, and then I would go home.

I found that Baas Jim was a very silent man. He would often sit alone on his stoep smoking his pipe, looking away into the distance. Sometimes his wife would sit with him. Even then there were long silences. I saw that there was great affection between this man and his wife. I was able to notice these things, as I often sat beneath the shade of a tree near the house cleaning harness and saddlery. I thought that one day I should sit at my own kraal, where Nondwe would be mistress.

All this time I had in my mind the little package which had been given into my charge. I had begun to be afraid of that package. I have said that Baas Jim was a stern man and I feared that when he read the contents, which were only partly known to me, he might fall into a rage and vent his anger upon me. You know, Nkosi, that when a man feels that his anger has been just, and he is reminded of the cause of that anger, he sometimes flares into even greater rage than he has felt before. So, Nkosi, I waited for a sign that the time was seasonable for me to fulfil my trust.

Nkosi, there is a time for speaking, and again there is a time for silence, just as there is a time for sleeping and a time for waking. The night is far spent, and I had forgotten that you must be weary with your long ride. Come, I will show you to your resting-place. In the morning we will talk again.

Good night, my Chief; sleep restfully.

21

The Fulfilling of a Trust

Good day to you, Chief. I hope that you have slept well. I see that you have already bathed yourself in the stream. What is it with you white people that you must always be washing yourselves? Is it that you are very dirty? With us we wash when we must, that is when we require to purify ourselves after touching a dead body or on account of some ceremonial which requires that one's body should be washed.

Come, Chief, and partake of this piece of broiled kid I have had prepared for you; stamped maize will go well with it – we have no bread. After you have eaten we will, if you wish, sit in the sunlight and talk. The rain has gone, and the smell of damp earth with warm sunlight upon it is good to one's nostrils.

You are reminding me, Chief, that I cut off my story when I was telling you of the little package and how I was waiting for a sign that the time for its delivery had come.

One day Baas Jim told me to prepare everything for a hunting expedition. I was to grease the wheels of the little wagonette; I was to see that the harness for the four horses was clean and in good order and have everything ready for a start at dawn next morning. I had learnt much at this farm. What pleased me greatly was that Baas Jim told me that I with two other servants would accompany him as after-riders.

We started at dawn and travelled most of the day, halting when the sun was hot to outspan and rest the horses.

In the late afternoon we came to the camping-place near a forest. We boys set to and built a lodge of branches and leaves for the master and his Nkosi-kazi; on the floor we strewed soft grass. Then we made the fire and one prepared the food for our white master and his lady.

After they had eaten, Baas Jim lit his pipe and sat silently looking out into the darkness. His Nkosi-kazi sat beside him. I was washing up the plates and dishes.

Now, Nkosi, you know that I do not speak your language well. While I understand almost all that may be said I hesitate to speak your language because I make mistakes, and those mistakes have sometimes been turned to ridicule. Nkosi, I do not like being laughed at, except perhaps when I have said something which I have intended to make you laugh.

I was at my work of washing up the plates and dishes. Baas Jim and his lady sat looking out into the darkness. The only sounds were the sounds of night – the passage of water over a pebbly bed, the sound of soft wind in the trees. Away in the distance a jackal cried, answered by his mate. I was careful that the plates did not strike upon each other as I washed and dried them – that would have made a noise that did not belong to this place.

I had almost completed my work and was about to ask Baas Jim if there were anything further he required of me before I went to my sleeping-place, when he broke his long silence.

I cannot repeat all that I heard at that time, nor can I remember the exact words of what that man and his lady said to each other, but it was something like this:

Baas Jim said: 'Hear that jackal calling away in the distance; hear the answer of his mate.'

Then there was silence between them. Baas Jim after a while went on, addressing his lady: 'Do you remember the time when Jack and I quarrelled? We had been hunting and had

140

camped on this very spot. As we sat smoking after our supper, jackals cried just as those two are crying now each from the very same spot. I wonder where Jack is, and what he is doing. I know he went to the mines, and that is all that I do know.'

Nkosi, this was the sign. I have not repeated the whole of what Baas Jim said, but it was clear to me that he had love in his heart for his brother.

I left my dishes and crept away into the darkness. From my smoking-bag I took the little package which had been given me by a man whose name I now knew to be Jack.

I returned to the fire and placed some dry brushwood upon it, so that it should blaze up and give a good light. Then with misgiving I slowly approached Baas Jim. I knelt before him and handed him the package, saying at the same moment: 'My Chief, extend your pardon to me.'

Baas Jim said: 'What nonsense is this, Ntsukumbini? What is the meaning of this dirty little parcel?'

I said: 'My Chief, the outside of the parcel is dirty, but I believe that within it you will find that which is white and cleansing. Read on, my Chief, and so doing extend your pardon to me.'

Baas Jim tore open the dirty wrapper and held the paper it had contained to the firelight. 'What is it, Jim?' said the Nkosi-kazi, who was holding closely to his arm. Baas Jim took no notice of this, but kept on looking at the paper. I saw him brush his eyes with the back of his hand, and then that hand sought its way to his bared throat.

Again the Nkosi-kazi said very gently: 'What is it, Jim? Tell me.'

Baas Jim with his hand to his bared throat swallowed with difficulty and, thrusting the letter towards his lady, said: 'My God, read that – dear old Jack!'

Still kneeling, Nkosi, I waited for the storm which might

break upon me. I had fulfilled my trust, but I knew little of the ways of white folk. Baas Jim seemed to have forgotten my presence when suddenly his eyes met mine. He sprang up and picking up a log of wood came towards me. He hissed between his teeth: 'Black swine, why did you not give me this letter before?'

Nkosi, I felt the blow upon my head before it had fallen, yet it never fell. There was a long silence, or it seemed to me to be long, and the thing that broke it was the clatter of the log as it fell from the hands of Baas Jim.

Oh Nkosi, the sound of the falling of that log was as of the bursting of cords which had bound me. I had threatened the life of a helpless, stricken man, and he the brother of the very man who in my need had befriended me. Things had now been made equal, and I was purged of the evil that I might have done.

Baas Jim strode off into the night; his lady sat by the fire, clasping and unclasping her hands, with bent knees and bowed head. I remained at the spot where I had handed Baas Jim the package.

I heard a step behind me, a strong hand gripped my shoulder. The voice of Baas Jim broke the spell: 'You may be a damned black nigger, but you are white right through' – the very words that had been spoken to me by his brother. I knew then that there was communion between these two whom years had separated.

Nkosi, there was no hunt in the morning. The little wagonette, according to the orders of Baas Jim, was inspanned at the grey of dawn, and we returned to the farm at a pace that cannot be described.

When we got back Baas Jim shouted at me to have a fresh horse saddled for him. This to me was the work of a few moments. I had the horse saddled and ready as Baas Jim came dashing out of the house. He flung himself into the saddle and he was away like the wind before his feet were in the stirrups – he had gone to seek his brother.

Nkosi, it is not for me to know of the affairs of those white people. I had performed that which I had been asked to undertake and I hoped that good might come of it. For me there the matter ended and I put it from my mind.

I applied myself to the work that had been set for me – the care of horses – and it seemed to me that the horses of Baas Jim under my hands worked better and looked better than they had done before. As very many years before I had liked the work of herding cattle because it was a work easily avoided, so as a grown man I liked the work of tending horses because I saw in them the result of my efforts, and the scant praise of Baas Jim was always pleasant to hear.

All the time that I worked at this place labourers came and labourers went. At the sheep-shearing period they were many; at the time of reaping they were many. Then the extra men that had been engaged for a particular season went their ways and we saw them no more; these comings and goings were part of the farm life. One permanently employed in a position of trust took not much heed of these passers-by; such people were in a way beneath the notice of those of us who hold the confidence of our master.

Then one day there came a man whose face was familiar. I looked at him while he returned my gaze, and then we recognised each other – it was Lesalla, whom I had met on the Drakensberg, the man who had helped us to dispose of certain cattle.

22

A Soothing Ointment

I was very glad to see Lesalla, not only because I liked him but also because I felt with his aid I would now be able to carry out a plan that I had been turning over in my mind all the time I had been at the place of Baas Jim.

Employment was found for Lesalla; he was to help me in the care of the horses. It was very pleasant to have a close companion in my work, and when the day's duties were over we spoke together, sometimes till late into the night.

We discussed the plan I had in my mind – this was to go to Rooi Piet's and take some of his horses.

When I showed Lesalla my back and told him the story of my stripes, he was eager to join me in the visit to the place of Rooi Piet. The undertaking was a difficult one and must be carefully considered and discussed. There was no need to hurry with it.

One day after Baas Jim had been away quite a while a cart drove up to the house. In the cart was Baas Jim and his brother, whose name I had learned was Jack. When they got out of the cart I saw that Jack limped badly. I knew that this must be the result of the accident in the mine. The sight of this man brought all that back to my mind very clearly. For some reason I cannot explain I was covered with confusion when I saw Jack, and the one thing I desired was not to meet him.

For a long time I managed to avoid him, then one day he

came upon me unawares. He looked at me long and in silence. There was that in his face which pleased me, but I hoped he would go away without speaking. He said: 'Come up to the house; I want to talk to you.' I followed him to the house. He sat on a chair on the stoep. I stood below him.

He told me that after he had been taken out of the mine he had told people about me, and had asked them to find me. They had found the dead body of Nyaniso, and owing to the likeness between us they thought it was I who had been killed. Great search was made for the third man, who they believed to be Nyaniso. No trace of him could be found, and his disappearance had never been explained.

Jack said he had lain in hospital for many weeks. At times his life had been despaired of; in the end he had completely recovered, except for the fact that he would always limp. He ended his story by saying that but for my aid he would never have left that mine alive.

For a while he was silent and there was nothing for me to say.

Then he spoke again: 'I struck you in the face, and after that you saved my life. That blow I shall regret till my dying day. What you did for me I can never properly repay. If you want money, it is yours; if you want cattle, you shall have them.' When he had finished he waited for me to speak.

I stood before him as one might stand before an equal. I meant no offence. A time had come, Nkosi, when one who believed himself to be a man seemed called upon to show his manhood. I said: 'White man, there are some things one may do for another that require no recompense. It is not every service that may be valued in money. Let there be no talk between us of payment for the things you say I have done for you.

'On that day we received many wounds. All I ask of you,

white man, is to remember that the blood which flowed from your wounds and mine is of the same colour. We black people have not the wisdom of white men; we are ignorant and often stupid; but remember that our feelings are much like your own. You sometimes wound our bodies, but more often you wound our souls. Chief, I thank you for your words of kindness.'

I saluted Baas Jack and was about to withdraw when he sprang up and grasped my hands in both his own. Nkosi, that hand-grip repaid me for anything I might have done for him.

For me that matter was ended there.

I looked about for Lesalla, and when I had found him I said that it was time we went about the business which would take us to the farm of Rooi Piet. There was that within me which craved for vigorous action and excitement.

We borrowed two horses from Baas Jim and obtained his permission to be away a few days. He wrote us a pass saying that we were his servants and had his horses.

It was a long way to the farm of Rooi Piet, but it was much more pleasant to travel on horseback than on one's own weary feet.

We got to the neighbourhood of the farm in the afternoon of the second day. We halted at a secluded spot away from the road and out of sight. Lesalla, being a stranger, went down to the homestead to pick up any news that might be useful to us. He pretended that he had come to seek work and learned that Rooi Piet was away at the village. This suited our plans very well.

We waited for nightfall, and then went to that part of the farm where the horses grazed. As we approached the troop they snorted and bounded away in the darkness. I whistled softly in a way known to them, when they stood timidly, ready to dash off again. We approached, softly whistling till we got right among them. I knew this troop of horses well, having, as I mentioned before, observed and handled them. In the dark it was somewhat difficult to select the two I required, but eventually these were caught and we set off, each leading one.

We had just got to the gate in the farm fence by which we had entered when we heard a horseman approaching. He was upon us almost before we were able to realise it. We had not heard him before, as the ground was soft and sandy. The man pulled up and peered at us and the horses, then with a bellow of rage he dashed up to me with uplifted sjambok. It was Rooi Piet!

Nkosi, I was too quick for him. I swung my stick and smote with all my might. The blow landed squarely on the top of his head at the instant his horse crashed into mine, almost unseating me. Rooi Piet fell to the ground with a thud and lay quite still.

We dismounted to examine the extent of his injuries. He had lost consciousness. The blow on the head had stunned him. Nkosi, you will never know the joy to me of that blow. As my stick struck Rooi Piet's head, the dull thud was pleasant music and I uttered a grunt with the effort of striking.

We took the reins off Rooi Piet's horse, and with these we bound him hand and foot, so that he could not move; then we dashed off into the night.

We travelled swiftly but cautiously and reached the farm of Baas Jim very late the next night. We took the two horses that had belonged to Rooi Piet and placed them in a remote part of the farm which was seldom visited. We got back to the homestead just as dawn was showing, before anyone was astir. Later on we reported ourselves to Baas Jim and resumed our ordinary duties.

The most difficult work in the disposal of the horses still lay before us – they might be discovered and unpleasant questions would result. Lesalla and I spoke long over this question. In the end it was decided that I should ask Baas Jim to release me from work and I would go off with the horses.

I went to Baas Jim and asked him to release me from service. He tried hard to persuade me to stay on. I said that there were important affairs at my home urgently requiring my presence there.

Baas Jim wrote me out a travelling-pass. I looked at this and said: 'Nkosi, I see that you have not mentioned my two horses in the pass.'

He said: 'What two horses are these – where are they, and where did you get them?'

I said: 'Nkosi, I am afraid I have acted wrongly. Without your permission I have kept them grazing on this farm. I bought these horses from a farmer. I paid for them long before I got them.'

Was this not the truth, Chief? Had I not paid for those horses with my blood?

Baas Jim looked at me in a puzzled way, and seemed dissatisfied with my explanation, so I continued.

'My Chief, I have told you that I bought those horses. I have served you faithfully since I have been at this place, and there is that between us which should make you know that I would not lie to you.'

Baas Jim still looked doubtful. Just then Baas Jack limped up to where we were and joined in the talk. I was very much tempted to tell of the way in which I had paid for the horses – they knew, of course, of the flogging I had received from a farmer, but they did not know that these horses had been taken in payment for my stripes.

In the end Baas Jack said: 'Do what the man asks. I believe he bought the horses.' I got my pass.

It was arranged between Lesalla and myself that I should

make for the kraal of his father, Morosi, on the Drakensberg, where I would hand over the horses. Lesalla said that the horses were clearly mine, and he would take no share whatever in the profits of the transaction. I protested against his generosity, but nothing would move him; he cut that talk short by going on to describe the safest and best roads by which to reach his father's kraal.

It took me many days to reach the kraal of Morosi. I was stopped from time to time by people who desired to see my pass. A glance at it satisfied them. In these days the matter of passes is a very difficult one. At that time a pass was an easy thing and there were fewer police.

I handed over the two horses to Morosi and at the same time gave him news of the welfare of his son.

In the morning the horses had gone. It was no affair of mine.

I remained at that place several days waiting for Morosi to speak of payment for the horses. Then one day a strange man came to the place. This man and Morosi retired into a hut, where they remained for a long time. When the man left Morosi called me to him and showed me £20 which he said was my share of the horses. We talked about that money for quite a long time. I said it had been my wish to return home driving cattle, not carrying money which people could not see.

In the end Morosi gave me four fine cows in the place of the money, and here was I taking dowry cattle away from the very kraal where I had long before desired to pay dowry cattle for the girl Mokhoatsi.

Morosi satisfied me that the four cows were his very own and that he had bred them, so I went without misgiving first to the Headman and then to the Magistrate and got a pass for my cattle. It was pleasant to be able to travel along openly with the things that were my own, yet my satisfaction received a shock.

As I was travelling through the country of the Silangwe clan, I passed near the kraal of old Ndumndum, of whom I have made mention. When near the kraal I heard a shout: 'Heyi, young man driving cattle, come here and give an account of yourself and your cattle.'

It was old Ndumndum who had called me. He repeated his order that I should give an account of myself. I showed him my pass and told him that I had bought the cattle with money from Morosi.

When I mentioned the name Morosi, Ndumndum sprang up, his eyes shot fire and his beard bristled. He said: 'I've caught a thief today. I have long been watching that old jackal Morosi who lives among the rocks, and I see that you are one of his people.'

I protested against all this, yet Ndumndum called up one of his men and told him to make haste, ride hard and fetch the police.

It seemed if the matter of my cattle were probed too deeply that some difficult questions would have to be faced. I asked Ndumndum to stay his messenger for a few moments while I gave a full account of myself and my cattle. I saw that this was the only thing to do. We two retired into a hut, where I told the old man the whole truth. I ended by saying, 'These four cattle are an ointment to heal the wounds I show on my back.' When I had finished, the old man, who had been a policeman, looked at me long and steadily. I knew that he was judging my case. His judgment was in my favour. He called to a young man to bring beer and he bade the men enter the hut.

He said: 'Men of this place, I have detained this young man with his cattle. I am now satisfied that the cattle are his own and that they have been bought with money he has earned in a very hard way; he may continue his journey in peace.'

Then the beer-pot was passed round.

Nkosi, I have no more to tell you of that part of my life.

I reached home proudly driving my four cattle and I had money upon me saved from my wages to buy three or even four more.

My parents received me with consternation mingled with the greatest joy. They had believed me to be dead.

There was a great gathering at our kraal of all our friends and neighbours. My father slaughtered a fat ox and beer flowed like water. There was much feasting, dancing and singing.

When the revelry was at its height I slipped away quietly into the night with Nondwe – Nondwe, my blue crane.

Ntenkumbini: (Cattle Thief).

1. Youthful days.

Chief of mine! It is kind of you to come and talk to an old man such as I am. My head is grey, my eyes are dim and my back is bent but when I speak to you of the old days I feel for the moment young again. Most of my old associates are dead and gone and many of the white men who knew me have also departed, so there is now no reason why I should not speak freely. What I may say is not likely to harm them in the place to which they have gone.

You say you intend to write down my words and put them in a book. What have I to do with writings and books?

The original manuscript's opening page
(courtesy of the Johannesburg Public Library)

CHATS WITH CHRISTINA

Foreword

All the characters figuring in this work are, or were, living people.

Christina who did the talking came of that section of the Nama tribes known as Griqua. After various migrations this section settled down in what is now known as the Orange Free State. While there they were offered territory in 'No Man's Land'. Their chief, Adam Kok, sent scouts to spy out the land, who returned reporting that it was 'delectable country'.

So Adam Kok and his people trekked across the Drakensberg into this 'No Man's Land'. They built a fort and established a township. Kok was acknowledged by one of the Cape governors to be an independent sovereign. He had his own parliament and ministers of state. This was about 1850.

Later difficulties arose between the Griquas and British administrators. As the outcome of what was called the 'Griqua Rebellion' in 1878, Kok was deprived of his sovereign rights. The whole position had been complicated by Griquas selling farms to Europeans. But this is not a history.

The Griquas are a merry people, delighting in song, dance and feast. Their men served nobly in the last war, as they have done in this one.

It is hoped that no serious injustice has been done to Christina in the recording of her 'chats'. Her mode of expression varied according to her mood. She had a way of clipping a 'g' and putting a 'k' in its place. She would sometimes add an unnecessary consonant at the end of a word. Her use of longer words was occasionally uncertain, but she was always able to convey a clear impression of what was in her mind.

1

A Faithful Servitor

A servant brought me word that an old Griqua woman wished to see me. I went out. There was the old lady wearing the national headdress of her people – a stiffly starched kappie – and an equally stiff and spreading skirt. Her spotless clothing smelt pleasantly of a recent laundering.

'Oh! Frenkie,' she said, 'I am so glad to see you again after all these hears. When I last seen you you was just a little feller so high. Don't you remember me? I am Christina, what used to look after you. This girl here, Rosaline, is my grandson's stepdaughter. That's wot he has always told me but I think there mus have been something wrong in his step. I never ask him about that. Anyway, she's a nice good girl under my suppression.'

When, lying politely, I professed to remember Christina perfectly well, I asked her and her stepgranddaughter into the house and showed them into the pantry. Tea and cake were brought. I joined in the feast, waiting for Christina to open up, as I felt sure she would.

'Yes, Frenkie,' she said, between mouthfuls of cake washed down by a gulp of tea. 'You was just a little feller then. Your mother Frances sent for me. She said, "I can't do nothing with that boy, he is so wistful, he does jest whatever he likes and no one to stop him, his father is away."

'I took on the job saying that my lawful grandson Johannes

would help me. You boys played together nicely. We watched you from under the thatch roof of the veranda of the big house. You two made clay oxen and little waggons with clay wheels.

'Frances, your mother, smiled. It was good to see that. She had been sick. I said to her, "Lady Frances, we can leave these boys to play together. It will be a weigh off your mine. You needn't worry." So between her and me we left it like that. Things went nicely.

'Then one day when we wuzzen looking you and Johannes went somewhere. When it came for time to go home, I called for Johannes, he wuzzen there, so I went home.

'When I got there I found Johannes laying on a bed. His two eyes was shut up and he couldn't open them. His mouth was like a bit of raw meat. His clothes was all wet.

'I ask how all this come about. Johannes said you had said he had stole your father's apples. "First he plasters me like this," he says, "then he threw me in the swimming pool to wake me up." Johannes said he *had* stolen the apples.

'The next day your father come home. I was there. He went down his garding to see how his apples was getting on. Below the tree he saw all his apples laying with pieces bitten out. The apples was green.

'Your father goes up to the house in a rage and looks for you. He gets you, takes a big strap and puts it acrost you. I was there. Your mother Frances was laying in bed sick. I knew the strap made a lot of noise but didn't hurt much. I winks at Frances. When you set up a yell, Frances says, "Charles, you are killing the child." So your father let up.

'If it hedden of bin for me, Frenkie,' Christina said, 'you would have been heng, jailed, berried and dead a lot of times, but one thing I like to remember is that you never told the old man that it was Johannes who had stole the apples, not you.'

Christina swilled the last sugary content of her teacup and

tossed it down.

'Can I come and listen to you talking on another day?' she said.

I said she would be welcome.

2

A Love Affair

'Yes, I seen the whole thing from the beginning to the ending of the day,' said Christina at our next meeting. 'It was a birfday or a holiday or Christmus or something like that.

'Anyway you gits hole of a plocket knife that belongs to one of your brothers older an better then you. Your dear mother Frances would not let you have a plocket knife of your own for of fear that you might commit murder or some other nuisince.

'The first thing I seen that day was you cutting at the stem of that very tree there and there I see cut FB; MC. You'd finished your dirty job when I come up, but I seen it. You drops the knife you ortento of had and you went up that tree like one of those yaller monkeys.

'You was singing a song as you hopped about the branches up there:

Christina,
Have you seen her?
If you want to ketch me
Come and fetch me.

'Now, I was never a tree clomber, but I knew you'd have to come down sometime, and you did. A branch broke and down you come. I caught you in my harms before you broke your head and neck and all that. You, you riffiand says, "Thank you, Christina, I jes wanted to give you a fright, I always come down trees backwards." Then I knew for certain you was born to be heng.

'Just then I see you trying to straighten out your close.

'There coming up the road was Mordie, that little girl you was very fond of, and I don't blame you. She was the MC wot you cut beside FB on the tree. Mordie used to come and try to learn about playing the pihannah, but it wuzzen your sister Hannah who taught her, it was your sister Ketsie.

'Well, this day when you fell out of the tree and broke your neck – except for me – you jes took Mordie by the hand and there you two loafers goes past the house and set on the grass behine the rose hedge.

'A little later your pa come riding up on that chestnit horse with a white bles, his name was Manel. I sez, "Good afternoon, Sir Charles." He wasn't a Sir really, but he ought to of bin.

'Now, your father was that tall he could see over the top of anything and by what I will tell you later you will know that he seen over the top of the hedge where you two loafers were setting on the grass.

'Why I say it must a bin a birfday or something that day was because I seen the white black mange with jam on it that was laying in the pantry and another thing was, your pa, Sir Charles, come into dinner with a white shirt front bigger en a winder.

'Sir Charles sets at the top of the table and asts a blessing. I can even remember that. He says, "Scanify this food for our uge and us to thy sewage." Behine Sir Charles was his two hunting dogs. The one as black as ink was called Sweep and the other, sort of red and white – I forget his name.

'Well, anyhow, the dinner perceded merry and bride till it come for the time of black mange with jam on.

'The pudding was dished out all round and jist then your father, Sir Charles, says to you: "Who kissed Mordie behind the rose hedge?"

'You looks at him in a rage, looks down at your plate of black mange with jam on, picks up the plate and lets your father have the lot on his white shirt front.

'Your father jumped up to give you a clout, but your mother Frances puts her gentle hand on his arm and sez, "Charles, you arst for it, the boy has spirit."

'Sir Charles, your father, sits down in his seat with the jam all over his shirt that I would have to wash. "Bring the boy some more black mange with a lot of jam," he says.

'That's the kind of people your parings was. The source of the evil was Mordie your loafer.'

3

A Bad Appetite

'Your ma Frances used to give you some maracine every now and then to keep your bowilds right. She come to me one day and sez: "The boy issen eating, looks to me as if he's goin to be sick." I sez to Frances she's thinkin thinks, there's no green fruit, anyways little boys might git of coller at times like anybiddy elst.

'But still, Frenkie, I keeps a dubble wash on you in case of acciderns. You goes to that little place nex the swimming pool. You was there quite a long time as fur as I noo and thort I would watch for you on your way back and waits. I seen the door of the little place open but you wuzzen there and wonder if you gorn back to the big house another way. I went down to the big house, you wuzzen there.

'It was gettin near midday meal time and I thort you'd turn up but you didden. I goes up to the plaze where the prison gang was takin their food to arst if they'd seend you. They was eating mealie porridge with a little sugar in out of a big pot. The prisonders was pickin it out with chips of wood from the wood pile.

'An there was you sittin among those malefactors dipping your chip in the pot and eating mealie pap along with them. You seem to like that kind of compny. I was that ashame, I didden know what to do. I makes a grab at you but you darts away and shets yourself in the fowld run.

'Having found out the secret of your bad appertide, I had to tell Frances somethink. I says that you was so sorry seeing those poor prisoners working so hard, it must of put you off your feet, that the geng should go and work somewhere elst.

'Well, anyhow Frenkie, the geng's job was finished in your pa's garding, they went to work somewheres elst and you got back your appertide.'

4

A Sore Throat

Sitting on our veranda, I heard a rustle of skirts. The sort of sound that has always stirred one. I looked down.

There was Christina.

'Ain't it Chewysday?' she said. 'My clock has just gone and stop and I wuzzen quite sure.'

I said it was Tuesday and she was right on time. We had arranged this day and time for our, or should I say, *her* next chat. A maid brought up a chair and later a table on which she set tea things.

It may not be realised that I was offering hospitality to royalty. Christina was closely related to Adam Kok who at one time was acknowledged to be an independent sovereign in that country. If you think my history is faulty, look up the facts. Anyway, the facts having been as I know them to have been, I treated Christina with a degree of deference and did not resent her use of Christian names.

Christina poured out the tea daintily. It was then that I noticed the shapeliness of her hands. We drank our tea and ate our cake.

Christina gathered up her skirts and shook away the crumbs that were there, then looked down the avenue of gum trees that stood before the house, as if seeking inspiration.

'Frenkie,' she said, 'do you remember the time you said you had a sore froat? I won't ask you about that because I knew jes as much about it as you did.

'I knew you hedden done your lessons and you was afraid to go down to Billy Tyson's school for fear of the hiding you might git. You went around croaking like a sick frog.

'Your mother ties an old stocking roun your neck and gives you a dose of honey and worm gall. You didden like it much.

'You was sitting there like a cherrybum as if nothing wooden melt in your mouth. Then your two elder brothers, elder and better'n you, comes clattering down the backyard. With them was the three worst scullions in the wole town. Their names was Nattie and Erbie and Billy.

'The only good feller in that bunch of scullions was their eldest brother, whose name was Plunket. He was a blacksmith. I always wondered where he got a funny name like Plunket. Then one day I was passing the blacksmith shop and saw this eldes brother of the scullions hitting a piece of iron with a heavy hammer. Every time he smote a smite, it went plunket, plunket.

'I thought quite a lot about that. His parings must of been a bit late about something, only giving his name Plunket when he was a grown blacksmith. But I lef it at that, never interfering with other people's interferings, at lease, not much.'

Christina poured herself another cup of tea and took another hunk of cake. Between chews and gulps she continued her story.

'I was going to tell you about this sore froat of yours when something interrumpted me.

'You sits there, as I said, like a little cherrybum until you hears your brother, older and better then you, with the other three fiends come clettering down the yard. When you heard them saying they was going for a bathe, you sets up and begins to pull at the stockin round your neck.

'Your mother says, "Frenkie, you mustn bathe today you

got a sore froat." This was the sore froat what helped you from getting a hiding from your schoolmaster, Billy Tyson.

'I'm not sure if you sez "No ma" or "Yes ma", but you keeps on setting down quiet for a while, jes like that same cherrybum.

'Then you sez to me, "Christina, take me for a walk, it may do my sore froat good", and we walks down between those very gum trees you see here. I didden have much suspicion. The nex thing was we was down by the ribber and there was those reptiles bathing naked. You sez to me, "Christina, I'll just rest in the shade behine this bush for a bit." The nex thing I knows was you in the water with the other reptiles.

'I thought I would go in and pull you out, but being a disrespectable married woman I couldn't take my close off in presents of a male company and I couldn't go in with my close on because several people would of been drown including me.

'Then it come to me. The Reffernd William Dower our pasturage had tole us, "If you meet with trials and tribulus put it to the Lord in prayer."

'I knew all about the prayer for rain, that didden fit in. I knew the prayer giving thenks, that was no good. Then there was one about forgiving sins. I had no sins, at lease not much so's that I could menshun.

'So I put those three prayers together in one and did the bes I could hoping that something would come out of the lot.

'While I was still wrastling, you, you little devil, turns up fully dressed and smiling.

' "Where you bin, Christina?" you says.

'I bin wrastling with the Lord for the sake of your soul, if you got one, I says.

'You'd clean forgot about your sore froat. I asks wot you gwine to tell your ma about this. You says, "I gwine to tell her just what happen."

'When we get home, your dear mother Frances was sittin and knittin. "Ma," you says, "you tole me not to bave, but I had to have just a little swim. There was a lot of wrastling, but Christina is not very strong about that. Anyway, my sore froat is better."

'"I'm sorry you disobeyed me, my boy, but I'm glad you tole me the trufe. Christina," she says, "give this boy his supper and put a lot of honey on his bread and butter, honey is good for a sore froat." That's the kind of Christian lady your ma, Frances, was. But me, I was boiling for the things you done me that day. I'd rather give you a clip of the year than put honey on your bread, but I done what I was tole.

'Yes, Frankie, you was a hard cash. I leaf you to my bread and honey.'

5

A Corrective

With a book on my knee I was dozing when I heard a slight insinuating cough. There was Christina. She asked if it was the right day and time. I said it was. I put a chair for her. She said her clock was going again.

'I like to hear you talking, Frenkie,' she said. 'It remines me of the olden times when you was a little feller so high.

'One day your mother said to me she would read me a bit out of a good book called *Pilgrim's Process* or something like that. She open the front page and there was the pitcher of a man carrying the biggest bundle of washing I ever seen. On the bundle as fur as could be seen was "sins". I spose on the other side was "wash" to make "washsins". I was your mother's washerwoman and was interest, but there was nothing about washing in what your mother read. It was all about a norrible man who done lots of bad things. Your mother reads on in her sweet voice and it was her fault if I fell asleep.

'When Frances close the book with a slap, I was wide awake in an instink. "Excuse me, Frances," I sez, "I better go and see what Frenkie is doing."

'I went down the garing and there you wuz sitting under a tree. There was bits of carrots and parsnips and turnips and some pits of green apricots. You'd been eating all these things. You didden even get up. When I arst you about it, you said you was getting food for the roberts lair and the other roberts might be there any time. You tole me the lair was in the stable loft and I might be shot any time.

'I didden wait to be shot, I had to get that poison stuff out of your stummick. I gets you by the back of the neck and takes you up to my room where I gives you a pergatory.

'I won't say any more about that, Frenkie, but nex day you was one of the tamest little boys I ever known. I think I save your life that day.'

6

The Grass Fire

'Even on a Sundy bad things ken heppen, Frenkie,' said Christina.

'This one Sundy I'm telling you about was communiond or yearly service, I ferget which. Your parings went down fust and tole me to see that yous come down about a arf hour later.

'There was you three in your white shoots looking like cherrybums. I'd washt and ironed those shoots and was proud of yous, except that I had to stop you, Frenkie, from chewing at the cornder of your lace collar. Apart from this there was something unrestless about.

'I was jest escoring yous down to the church when a grass fire comes raging down the hill, and up the street comes a bunch of prisners with a couple of perliecemen to put the fire out. They had branches and wet bags. That was the lars I seen of you merchands for a wild. The fire got bigger and the smoke thigger. Yous three got branches and joint the prisont geng to put the fire out. I coulden stop yous.

'Paul and Bout was spending their weekend in jail in that room your pa kep for them. They was just recovering from a Saturdy night. I check a bucket of water over them and tole them they must come out at once and riscover the master's children.

'Those two woke up quick, gets branches and joins the fire sweepers in the smoke. I was close behine them. Where there wuzzen smoke there was bits of fire. The tail of my dress got mixt with one of these en I had to put my ownd fire out. I sets down in the water furrer and then joins in the chaste.

'Soon after that the fire was put out but there was a lot of smoke about and I coulden fine yous for a bit. Then when I sore yous I didden know who you wuz – that black and dirty, I give in.

'When your pa and ma come home from church they coulden belief their eyes. They thought yous three had been up in the geldry where you been tole to go.

'I didden say a word. Your pa looks you up and downd. "What have you got to say for yourselfs," he says.

'Your eldest brother better looking, but no bettern you, stands up and says you'd been helping to safe your house and home from destrucshun by fire. When you was jest on your way to church the grass fire come down. Your pa shakes his head but says nothing.

'The nice Sundy dinner I had help to cook was eet in silenst.'

7

Hunting

'I tole you, Frenkie, that bed thinks could heppen on a Sundy,' said Christina. 'This was one of the worse.

'You know those two, Paul and Bout, I tole you about. If they wuzzen drunk they wuz in jail and if they wuzzen in jail they wuz drunk. But between times, now and then, they was quite nice fellows. They spent mose of their time in that little jail your pa kep ready for them at the big house. Whenever they was convict of something they went straight to your pa's little jail without no guard. When they get there they would get out their spades and dig in the garding to do the hard labour put on them.

'That's where Paul used to tell you Hottentot stories, while he was resting, and those two used to res quite a lot when your father was at his office trying culpricks.

'One day you comes up to that jail with a little bow and arrer you made. Paul says he'd make you a real good bow and arrers, it jist wanted a little terbakker to help him. He got the terbakker somehow. You might know something about that. Anyways, the making of that bow and arrers took a long time.

'Your pa comes in one day to fill his pipe. There was hardly any terbakker in the tin. Frances says, "Charles, I always say you smoke too much." So you got away with that.

'That bow and arrers was finished made on a Saturdy and Paul given them to you. Paul and Bout was always allow to go

172

down to the big jail Saturdys and Sundys for a res. There you was left alone with these free arms. The fowlds had a reckless time but you didden do much demmige on them. Then one of the kets comes along and you lets drife, hitting the ket in the hine leg. The ket goes off with the arrer dangling. I jest puts it to the Lord in prayer and the arrer drops orf.

'It's jest about supper time and the kets noo about that. Your pa says why does that ket keep on licking its hine leg. I sez it was a good sign, kets always keep on licking themselves when rain's coming. So you get away with *that*.

'The next day being Sundy you says you didden feel well, could you jest lay down and res. Frances says she spose you'd been eating yet more green fruit and it would be better if you was nearer to things.

'You lays downd as if you had a bad stummick ache, lef in my charge.

'My grandson-in-law, Johannes, turns up an I arsts him to watch over the sick while I went to see Maria about something and this is what Johannes tole me about it. He sed no sooner had I got down the street then you sed you was feeling better. You whistles up your pa's two hunting dorgs and sez, "Let us go hunting, Johannes, I got a bow an arrers."

'Those two dogs lays beside the bed where you was laying. That black one, Sweep, you tole him was a thief an stole every think he could lay his hends on. He said your pa caught him in the ac of stealing butter out of the safe and give him a hiding. Your pa holes him down and says, "Who stole butter, who stole butter?" All you had to say after that was "Butter, Sweep", if you wants to git the dorg out of the house. It comes out that you give your pa a coupler kicks in the shinds for beating that dorg.

'Anyways, you and Johannes with those two dorgs goes out hunting with your bow and arrers. You shet some birds and you put them in the pockets of your Sundy shoot.

'By the time your parings got back from church you was laying in bed. Johannes had put your Sundy close in the cupboard. You said you was feeling a little better, when your parings asked. The two dorgs was laying outside the door. Your pa says, "Looks if these dorgs bin out somewhere."

'It took some time for that affair to broil up. Juring the week Frances says, "Charles, there must be a dead mice somewhere." Your pa moves things about and sez he could smell somethink but cudden fine it.

'Then the nex Sundy come. Your bes shoot was got out and there was those birds in the pockets as had been there for a week. The whole thing come out, you got something but the worst punigment you got was being made to go to church in the oldes shoot you had – the loafer Mordie would be there.

'As I sed bad things can happen event on a Sundy. There was that grass fire on a Sundy, you breaks the sabber by hunting birds on a Sundy and you gets foun out on a Sundy.'

8

The Hailstorm

Christina took off her kappie, removed her hairnet, pushed back her thick frizzy hair and pointed to the mark of a scar.

'Do you know who done that, Frenkie?' she asked. I shook my head and was about to say something.

Christina proceeded. 'It was you done that on me, not exactly, but troo you.

'Do you rember the hailstormb? If you doan rember that you won't rember anything till Judgmin Day. I'll jes remine you, so'st you'll be able to answer true on that Day.

'It was like this. I was setting with Frances on the veranda, the sky turns as black as hing. There was a big stormb coming. Frances says, "You better see where the boys are." I finds those two older'n better'n you, doing lessons or somethink, at lease they said they wos, you wos not to be foun. Then I rember you said that you was going to see how Aubrey was getting on stinking a well. This Aubrey was another brother of your loafer Mordie. When I gets to Aubrey's place he was coming out of the well he been stinking. He sez he hedden seend you. I asked if Mordie was there, he said he didden know. I somehow thort yous wooden be fur apart.

'Then the first hailstone out of that storm drops on Aubrey's roof with a zonk louder'n a coupler bricks. I had to find you and remembers the empty house acrost the street where you and Mordie used to play.

'Jest then three men on horses comes up the street riding hard to git away in front of the stormb, en it was then the storm brake. Going acrost the street I see through a winder of the house you and Mordie holding ea chether, dead skeert of the noise on the roof, the hail was falling that heavy it might be a preserpist. Jest before I gets to the house one of those hailstones hits me on the head and knocks me out, the nex one brings me roun and I gets into the house. The noise on the tin roof was something orful.

'Then the storm stop as soon as it begun and the sun come out. I deliver Mordie safely to her parings. Those three horses I seen going up the street come back mad like, nobiddy was setting on them. I dunno what heppen to the riders.

'Then, Frenkie, I takes you home. There was Frances knitting as calm as could be. "I knew it would be all right, Christina," she says, "and worriting doan help, thank you."

'Now here's a thing, that big house was full of birds. I asks Frances about this. She sez, before the storm brake, the birds comes tapping at the winders, looking for shelter. She opens all the winders and in they come, in their hundreds. I can't help thinking they were looking for Frances.

'The nex day dead birds was laying thick under the trees. Our boys went an fetch them in thousands in buckets and bags. That was the hailstormb and this mark I shows you on my head is what I got out of looking for you in the hailstormb.'

9

The Grand Ball

'You may not rember all this for reasons I will tell you later, Frenkie.

'Whenever a noo store was opened and before the fixings was fixed a dance was given in that store wether the ownder like or not. It become a sort of ruled.

'The newest an biggest store was being opened and the Cape Infantry gave it out that a Grand Ball was to be given there. They fixt the ownder of the shop by telling him the store coulden be open till the ball had been held. The ownder of the store knew the Cape Infantry and had to say it be orrite, he knew he coulden open up if he didden allow the ball.

'The gels all got busy making noo dresses. When I had any spare time not looking after you I went roun to visit Katrina, Maria and the res to see how the young ladies was getting on. I even help them a bit trying on – hitching up here and pinning up there. I did my bes making those dresses. The bes of the whole lot was the one made for Miss Minnie, you know who I mean. When I seen her in that dress I sez to myself if she doan get merrit out of that costumbe she wooden be merrit ertall. I helped en she did. She became engage the very night of the ball and married a good feller. I was at the wedding and Donal her father takes me aside and says there was a little somethink in the pentry for me. There was and I fount it.

'But, Frenkie, I was meaning to tell you where you come

in all this when the maid interrump by bringing this tea and cake …

'Now, you three merchands decide to go to the ball and sent you to your ma to arst about it, you being the one that could twis her roun your thumb. Frances sighs and says she spose it be orlright, if I was there to keep order. She gives me a bob. I wanted to go to the ball to see how all the dresses I made would look.

'I puts a hot ironed over my bes dress and kappie. Carts turn up with officers for your three sisters who looked charmbing in what I made for them. I was put in a back seat of a cart with you three. The officer didden look too pleasured about it. Anyway, we get there. I kep you three under my harm.

'The bend of the Cape Infantry started, gentlemen took their pardners. So the ball begun and went on with polkas walzes mazurkans and all that. It was nice to see the red coats all mix up with the dresses I made and Miss Minnie was the belt of the ball.

'After a wild you went off to sleep and I reckons things would be safe for a bit. I doze off and when I woke up there was you in the middle of the floor, dancing what you called the Highland Skotshie, getting in everybody's way. Your sisters look sort of shame and one of them sez, "Carn't you do somethink about it?"

'One of the officers ketches you, picks you up on his soldier and sez, "Would you like some lemonade, Tommy?"

'You agrees to that. The officer takes you into the bar. You gits your lemonade. That officer takes you into a dressing room and lays you down on some coats hung up on the floor. I went to see you and you was fast asleep.

'Those two brothers of yours had gone home, sort of fade up with the ball. I thort it would be orlright fer a bit wild you sleep. Then I thort it was time I took you home. I went to the dressing room, you wuzzen there. I search all aroun and you wuzzen there, then I raises the mew en cry.

'You was foun drunk as a fiddle, laying in the water furrer. When we tried to take you out you started fighting, saying you was going to sleep the night there.

'We gets you home somehow. I scrubs you down, puts on your red flanull nightshirt, and gives you some maracine I had for sich cases.

'I doan know what that officer put in your lemonade but you smell very strong of gin when we rescue you out of that water furrer.

'Can you belief it, Frenkie, you was the first to git up in the morning. It mus have been my maracine. You tells your ma it had been a gran ball. There was no questions arts or incrimeraging statements made, so you gets away with it, as you always done. Your three sisters was still asleep.'

10

An Alarm

'There was a lot of Kaffir Wars in those days, Frenkie,' said Christina, 'as I tole you before. But your pa kep on stopping them before they become dangeroust.

'Anyways, a big sod wall was build round the ole church. All you boys help and the school was close. You all had red stuff tie roun your hets to show that you was good and loyal troops. You three merchands pushes barrers pulls carts and otherwise gets in pipple's way. I doan think you got any medals for that, but you mean well, besires the school was close.

'When the wall roun the ole church was build you had your holiday, Billy Tyson too, and you didden want to go back to the Public House School, you wanted to keep being in the army.

'You rember that big feller Eric, son of the Colonel. He says he'll make you into a proper regimen. He gits you down in that big field jes below the big house and drills you and drills you and makes you march till you was about dead bean. There mus have been about twenty of yous. Then yous got a bit less.

'Eric tells yous that desertion from the army is shertun death, and makes you dig a big place in the groun he calls it a guardvan. You puts a top on it made of weeds and things. Eric parades his regimen and says anyone foun guildy of linkering or desertioning would be put in the guardvan on pin of death. This Eric had got hole of an old baynet and you was dead skeert of that.

'You was the firs to be put in the guardvan. It may have been for linkering or because you didden bring down enough dried carrots for the troops, anyways there you was in the guardsroom on pin of death.

'That beautiful girl Phemie, Eric's sister, and me was watching all this over the top of the sod wall. When the regimen was on what Eric calls a root march, Phemie gets on top of the wall and signs to you to get out of the guardshole and go home. You did and that's how you came to leaf the army. The rest of yous finding soldiering too hard leafs the regimen in ones and two so's there wuzzen any more lef.

'I may tell you, Frenkie, that this same Eric become an officer and fought in a lot of those wars. Miss Phemie told me something about that ...

'What was you telling me about? Oh yes, it was about the wall roun the church that yous made. They said it was a fort and it was give out that if the Cape Infantry blew their bugles in the night that there was a Kaffir War coming on. Evrybody was to salad into the fort. The ladies and children was to go into the vestuary.

'One night the bugles did blew.

'Those two fellers, Paul and Bout, was a bit soberer that night. They was more soberer when I check some cole water on them and tell them to inspan the cart at wunst and rescue the fambly from the war. They done it quite quick. Those two big grey horses, name Pompey and Greaser, didn like being inspan in the middle of the night and they was a bit unressless. But I knew they was safe with Paul holing the reins. I bunnels you all into the big cart and me too.

'Bout says he stay behine and help the guards looking after the house. In those days there was always a lot of guards looking after the big house.

'Anyways, Paul gits us down to the church and we go into

the vestuary. I never seen such a side. There was mothers feeding their unbornd babies, there was Allie's ma with the wallpapers in her hair and all yous crowding in. Your ma tole me to take all of yous boys in the church. I done so and wen back to the vestuary.

'The thing that made me a bit weary was the fac that, saying nothink about Nattie and Erbie and Billy, that feller Allie was with you. I hear some sly souns coming out of the church and went to see. There was yous playing hide and creek between the spews. I restore order and goes back to the vestuary.

'Then I hear some more souns and went to see. Allie was setting at the harmondium and as he begins to start it, he says, "We will begin this servige with psalm Three Hundred and Ninety Seven." I cudden help it. I give him a clout and tells him to keep quiet and come down out of the galdery with me. He comes down and sets quiet in a spew. There was quiet for a wild but to make sure I goes back to make shertain.

'There was Allie in the pulpit. He was saying, "Finishing and lastly, berloved brethren – " He bangs the big Bible shut as me and his ma comes in.

'The wallpapers in Allie's ma's hair stood on hend. She says, "Allie, don't you know that you might be struck dead, with your throat cut, at any momen?"

'"Yes, ma," he says, "I knew all that, but I been trying to convert these heathens."

'It was jes then that an officer of the Cape Infantry come in. He says, "Sorry, ladies, it was a falst alarm. You can all go home now in safety. The carts are outside."

'The only bad thing about *that* alarm was that, when I get yous all safely home, I went to the cupboard in the cornder to see if I could get a little tonig after all I bin through. The square bottle was empty. Bout been guarding the house.'

11

The Magic Lantern

'Yes,' said Christina at our next meeting, 'I always said you was born to be dried heng en berried a lot of times and this night I'm going to tell you about it nearly happen.

'There was to be a magicalentring in the schoolroom next to the old church and it was said that pitchers of the Holy Land would be shown by a person who would tole you all about that country. All were invited free for nothing.

'Your mother Frances said you and your brothers oldern bettern you could go, but she gives me a bob and said, "Christina, I think you better go and stand in the backgroun, jes to see that nothing heppens to those boys."

'I puts out your bes shoots and then gives yous your suppers. You was all that excited about this Holy Land that you couldn hardly eat, scavengers as you was. What I give yous, yous swallers hole. Then yous sets off for the Holy Land. I let you go and follows at an indiscrief distance behind. Your ma Frances had tole me to keep a weary eye on you.

'You boys goes into the Sundy school and mixes with your mates, Nattie Erbie Billy and a lot of other barberiands. Wot made me keep my weary eye open, as your mother Frances said I mus, was the fac that among yous I seen that awfullest feller, Allie, again. You see, Frenkie, his pa and ma kep him down trying to bring him up a decent Christian and they had a hard way of doing it. They kep him down in a way boys shoulden be kep down, so when Allie got a charnst of getting out he was all out. This was his night out. Then the show begun, with pitchers – Jerusalem, Jordan River, the Dread Sea, Palestimes and so on.

'All this time I wuz keeping a weary eye on Allie, who so fur had set puffectly quiet looking at the pitchers. Then the magicalentring ended. I set in the backgrown watching wot yous boys would do.

'There was with you when you come out that horrible feller, Allie. He wuzzen any horribler than other small boys. He was full of beands, as you might say, and his parings try to make him into some kind of Christian woulden allow him to let them out.

'Now when yous come out of the magicalentring there was that nice boy Harry, other brother to your loafer Mordie. He always made people larf – even me. This Harry pulls out a tin whistle from his pocket and starts to play a chune.

'Then Allie sez, "Let's be the bend of the Cape Infantry." There was some empty tins laying about. Yous was the drummers and so yous went up the street, beating on those tins with Harry playing his tin floot. Allie was conducting the bend with a knobkerrie.

'Allie sez, "Let's give old Demmit some music."

'There the bend halts in front of Demmit's house. Then the music started, Harry in front with his floot and yous at the back with your tin-cans.

'Now, I must tell you, Frenkie, that nex to your farther Sir Charles, this man Demmit was the most important person in the town. He was the Chief Con*stable*. That's where he should have bin: grooming horses, rather than getting pipple in trouble.

'After your bend started, Mr Demmit comes out in a long night gownd. He blous his whistle.

'Some police come up and, on Demmit's orders, you are all surmounted and taken to the charge office. Can you belief it? I was there.

'I runs to your mother Frances, faster ever'n I run before. I makes a full report of the proceedings.

'You mus be tired of talking to me, Frenkie,' said Christina, 'I'll tell you the res of this thing on another day. Praps in my house, if you could find it probable to come there.'

I said I would be glad to 'come there'.

12

More about the Magic Lantern

On a day appointed I went down to Christina's thatched cottage, knocked at the door and entered. The earthen floor had been freshly smeared. There was a sweetness about the place that one could hardly have imagined. The cloth on the table was snowy white; on it stood a vase of flowers of some sorts.

I was received by Rosaline, Christina's stepgranddaughter-in-law. She smelt of scented soap. 'Grandma will be here in a minnit,' she said. 'Set down.'

Christina came in a moment later, her wide white skirts crackling with starch, her hairnet set 'just so'.

Rosaline brought in a teatray with a plate of scones. I knew of Christina's cooking and had no fears. We settled down to it.

'What was you telling me when we larst met, Frenkie?' she asked. 'Yes, now I remember, it was something about the lightringlangtrin, when you was all put in jail and when I went up foot hase to report to your mother Frances. She says to me: "Those boys must be release at once. It is horders."

'I runs jes as quick as I ken and looks this feller Demmit in the face when I got in his office. I sez to him, You jes release these boys now, it's horders of the big man at headquars. I knew he wuzzen at home, but I thought a little lie like that might help your mother Frances.

'This man Demmit blinks his eyes and says, "All right, Christina, take them away. But they will have to come before the court for distributing the peace. I got all their names and addresses and when I send for them and they aren't before the court it's you that will be put in jail."

'Thenks for your fret, Mr Chief Con*stable* Demmit. The boys will be before the court when summonsed, I sez, but give me a bit of paper, I jes want to make a note or two so's I won't fergit.

'He gives me a pencil and paper and I writes. "Wot you written, Christina?" he asks. I shows him: This here Chief Con*stable* Demmit has freatened to put me in jail for something I haven done, not yet.

'Demmit crumples up the paper and throws it in a baskit. "Get out, you witch," he says.

'I replies, I'm not a witch, or any other kind of dorg. There's now two more charges again you: abusive langwidge and throwing away court papers.

'Demmit was that wild he jumps up and comes towards me with cleaned fists. I gathers up my skirts, shakes my tail in his face with a sort of waggle and goes off knowing that the battle had been wond. I done all this for the sake of your mother – we all loved her. For her sake I was prepared to be an innicent incarcertraged criminal.

'That was the end of the matter so fur. We jest sits and waits to see what Demmit would do nex.

'But, Frenkie, you bin talking for a long time and must be tired. I'll tell you about the rest of this epishod another time.'

13

The Trial

'Is this the right day?' asked Christina. 'You see, my clock is jes like some pibble, it sometimes goes slow and then gits a bit too fast. I know about pibble but I don know much about clocks.'

I told Christina that this was the day and she was right on time. I think Rosaline, who was a very intelligent girl, must have kept her up to the mark. Not that Christina was ever late for a chat.

Rosaline disappeared into the house – she knew her way about – and very soon she and our maid came out with a table on which tea things were placed.

'What was you telling me about the larst time?' asked Christina, as Rosaline poured out the tea. 'Yes, I rember now. It was about that man Demmit. His name sounds like a curze, anyway it was his name and it serves him right.

'Well, we wuz all waiting to see what Demmit would do. Then one day a constable brought summonses for all yous boys to be at court to answer a charge of being righteous in a public thorofear. Some of your mas and pas was jes mad about the whole thing. Being a spare day orf, I went round to hear wot was being said.

'Now you boys hed all been drill by that feller Allie who said he was going to be the foment of the jewry when the case came on and that you was jes to take your cube from him. You had some meetings in the roberts lair in the stable loft where you had put a supply of dried carrots and turnips to feed the roberts.

'On the day of the case the court was croud. The young men of the place come to see what would happen. None of them liked Demmit because he wuz always trying to ketch them out on their innercent miscreants.

'I was there in court and could have got up and killed Demmit when I seen you poor little fellers standing up in a row as frighten as rabbits – that is, all excep Allie.

'Then a door opened and the Magistrate came in. His name was Wild, but he wuzzen like that, he was a kind Magistrate. Demmit shouts "Order in court". All the pibble stands up and then sits down as Mr John Truro Wild sits on the bench – that what they call it, but of course you mus know that.

'After that Demmit says what had happen after the maginelantring and how yous had been uprorous in a public thoroughfear.

'Mr Wild puts a henkerchief to his mouth to hide something and looks at some papers. "You are all charge with being drunk and righteous in a thoroughfear. Are you guilty or not?"

'Allie, who'd made himself foment of the jewry, says in a loud voice, "Not Guilty". He waves his arm to the lef and the res of yous start singing, "And so say all of us".

' "Order in court," shouts Demmit.

'By that time Mr Wild the Magistrate was wiping his eyes. "Do you mean to tell me," he sez, "that these little boys was drunk?" he sez to Demmit.

' "The word drunk may have got into the char by mistake," Demmit replies.

' "The char is withdrawn," says Mr Magistrate Wild. "The accuse are found not guilty."

'It was when I seen the Magistrate go off into his room

with a handkerchief to his face that I heard him laugh loud and long.

'But yous barbariands hadn't finished with Demmit.'

14

Retribution

Christina's cottage was separated from our house by a couple of fields. Seeing a white-clad figure on the cottage stoep, I went down to pay her a visit. There was Christina, sitting on a chair with folded hands in perfect repose. She made a picture that Rembrandt would have painted. I hesitated, not wishing to disturb her – was passing, but Christina saw me.

'Frenkie,' she called, 'I jes knew you was coming down to see me. Rosaline has got the tea things ready, that shows I knew.'

I sat down. Rosaline brought out a small table. On it she placed the tea things and a plate of those priceless scones that only Christina could bake.

'You was telling me, Frenkie,' said Christina, 'about the court case after the maginlantring business. When yous get out of court that feller Allie takes commarnd and lines yous up. "Bend forward," he sez and that nice boy Harry comes out with his tin whistle, that's the chap who was brother to Mordie the loafer. Up to then Harry had stuck the whistle in the back of his pants for fear of being arst about it, but when yous paraded, he comes forward, one to the front, as they sed in the Cape Infantry.

'Then Allie marches yous up the street, first halt wuz in front of Demmit's house, where you gives him a bit of music, and then Allie breaks up the parade. He'd had his day out.

'But I knew something bad was going to happen to him when he get home, so I follows quietly at a discern distance and when I gets to the house I sets and listens somewhere nearby. I heard Allie's mother who was a fierce woman say, "You have brought this house into disrepuge and you must sruffer for your misdeeds." Then I heard the hiding and Allie's howling.

'I couldn stend it. I went straight into the room where Allie was being torshered. I had my skirts gathered up. What's all this noise, I sez – is the house on fire or something?

'Allie's parings holes their hands and Allie darts out of the door. Wait for me at the duck pond, I says as he passed by. I jes shook my skirts in the face of Allie's parings and went to the duck pond.

'There I took down his trousis and I see evidence of a fierce hiding. I was going to wash the wouns when Joe the Indian barber come along. "What's it, Christina?" he arsts me. I knew Joe well. By some mistake he got married to a cousin of mine. I told him and he and me takes Allie to the barbourous shop. There Joe smears something on his tail. Allie was still sighing and sobbing like that song, but when Joe put the stuff on his tail he stop.

'I took Allie back to his parings. I shook out my skirts when I seen them and said, If this is the way you want to make your boy in a good Christian, you got it all wrong. I shakes my skirts again and went out.

'After that Allie was allowed a lot more libertine.

'So there was now two things to be revenge: that wuz old Demmit running yous in and Allie gitting his unjist hiding.

'You all went to see James – James, who worked in the shop of Williams and Co. You always went to see James for advice when you wuz in some trouble or deviltry. James was a very nice man, a man of peach.

'You went to James in a sort of depushun. "What you been up to?" he arsts.

'"We jest want to get a couple of things fixed up," one of yous sez.

'James hears all you has to say. Me too, I was in the shop arging about the price of peppermens. That arge took a long time so I heard, quite by acciden, all yous says to James and wot he says to you.

'In the end James says, "Get yourselves up into a respectable Nigger Bend. I'll teach you the singing and your mothers and sisters will make your close. You can go up the streets and make as much noise as you like. I'll get the Magistrate's permishun."

'One of yous arsts if you could sing in fron of Demmit's house. James smiled and sez you could.

'That's how you reckoned to get square with Demmit and so your Nigger Band was started. You had a lot of rehearsals in James's office and I bought a lot of peppermens in the store, just by acciden like. The man in the store asked why I was buying so many peppermens and always arging the price. I sez that my stepgranddaughter-in-law was suffering a lot from wind in the stummick and me too and peppermens was good for the wind. That's how I come to know all about the bend you got ready for Demmit. You see James's office was quite close to the counter where I was buying peppermens.

'Yes, Frenkie, it was jes by acciden that I come to know all about that bend.'

I reckoned that this was enough for one day and made a getaway.

15

Rehearsals

'Mr James who work for A H Williams and Co had a good deal of trouble gitting you in some kind of order. He was very perticler. All you merchands wanted to be in the bend. James calls you up by ones and three for a text. That feller Harry comes out with his tin floot and James passes him as effidgient. You see, James was very fond of Harry's sister oldern Mordie. I'm not saying anything again Harry or his floot but I think Mordie's sister had somethink to do with it.

'Nattie Erbie and Billy says they was dancers. They stamps their feet and wiggles their tails and James passes them.

'You three comes up as a triplet and sings a coupler songs, Pore Ole Jones and Darkies Lead a Snappy Life. James passes you. He had to, you being the sons of the big man at the top of the town.

'There was lef that feller Tom, who Jimmie Walsh flatten out and his misable brother Henry. They said they could sing a juet about old dog Trade.

'James looks at them as if he had a nasty tasde in his mouth, but he give them a charnst. And this is what they sang:

Old dog Trade is avver faceful
Old dog Trade is avver kind
He's faceful and he's kind
And his tail sticks up behine.

'Here James hits on the table with his little stick. "I carnt understan what you trying to sing," he sez. "What you mean, avver faceful?"

'Tom says, "Old Trade must of been fighting and that's where he got it."

'James side a long breathe and said, "Orrite."

'This time Tom got a faceful from Jimmie Walsh. I'll tell you about that on another time, if you and me don' fergit.

'There was a lot of these rehearsals. I was usually absint, buying peppermens and condemned milk or something in A H Williams and Co Store when they take place. That's how I come to know what was going on.

'These two, Tom and his misable brother Henry, goes on practising their song about old dog Trade. The way they sung it you would think they was going to a funeral. James try to brighten them up a bit, but no good, it was jes the same. They must of been tort it by their ma who was always having a lot of babies.

'Anyways, James gets over it like this. He puts in the programme: "The song, Old Dog Trade, will be sung by these two pallbearers who was present when the ole dog died." Funny enough, this song went quite well when the bend went out. The pibble thought it was mean to be a funny song.

'The rehearsals went on for quite a long time.'

16

The Band

This is what Christina told me at our next meeting:

'What with buying peppermens and absurd drops – both good for the wind – I come to learn that yous was going to have a dress rehearsald, so when I heard the band struck up led by that nice fellow Harry with his tin whistle, I jes wanders roun and at a time I thought was rife I somehow gets into James's office, saying I had left somethink I had lose somewhere and it might be here.

'James, always perlight, says, "Sit down, Christina, what have you lose?" I said it was somethink but I forget what it was. He says we'll find it for you, but meantime listen to this. James taps a stick on his table and yous, who was all out in the wool store behine the office, comes out and lines up.

'James waves that same stick and then I hears the sweetest thing I ever heard like that – children's voices singing. I may say that some of you was biggish children.

'You sung your corest and you all goes back to the wool store. Then James says the next item will be the clarnet solo. Out comes Harry with his tin whistle. I didn like it much but he done his best on what he had.

'There was a lot of other songs and things. I seen it through, but I was waiting for the night when the real stuff would be done.

'That afternoon I sez to James couldn I help. He says you

jest the person I want. I went down to the office on the day he sed and you merchands turn up one after the others, all got up like nothing I ever seen before. You all had high collars, black tailcoats and red trousis – all this clothing was made out of cheap stuff by your mothers and sisters. You all look a bit self conshuns as you goes into the wool store at the back of the office.

'Then James give me some black boot pollidge and sez, "Blacken their fazes."

'What, I sez, it's like you arsting me to commit wistful murder. I sez I'd only do it on condishun that I was made a member of the band.

' "What can you do?" he arsts.

'I fleps my skirts and spins roun a couple of times on one foot.

' "That's jes what we want," he sez, "a prima donas will set the whole thing off." So they accepted me as a prima donas in that Nigger Bend.

'It was not jest that. I knew I had to keep a weary eye on yous and that's the way I done it. I told my stepgranddaughter-in-law, Rosaline, she must be my trained bearer and showed her jest how to do it. At first she lifted my train a bit too high, but we put that right.

'When James seen me coming in with a wide wintry costumbe and Rosaline holding it up behine, he jest corfed and corfed. I done a thing that was quite nice of him, but I forgive him because I knew he had a bad cold nearly allwis, I think there was something very wrong with his chess.

' "That's just it, Christina," he sez. I gives him a couple of parakeets and James, who kep on coffin, said, "That's fine, Christina." Then I knew I was final instal in the bend.

'But I wanted to do something more as a try on. There was jest time. I nips orf down to my cottage and gits hold of

Johannes, my grandstepson-in-law. I gets a hard black bolder hat, a big pair of shoes and a long black coat. These belonged to the church virgin who was in jail for borrering some of the colleckshint. I quickly puts these close on Johannes and then we goes hate foot to A H Williams and Co.

'When James seen Johannes he asks what it was all about. I said Johannes was my page. I said if you had a train you had to have a page like they sez in the pitsher books. Besides, I sez Johannes will be the tax collector – that bolder hat will be the colleckshin plate.

' "That's an idea," says James, "I hadn't thought of collecting money."

'What, I sez, after all this trouble and palarker, are we going to sing to the pibble free and gracious?

'James excepts Johannes as a member of the bend as my page and tax collector.

'When all things was ready, we salaged fort into the street. That fellow Allie took commarn. Edie, his clever sister, helped him to get away under the noses of his parings. She said Allie had gorn to bed with a bad heddick and wanted to be quiet, but his ma, always suspicious, went to see. There was Allie lying in bed, holding his head groanding. This clever sister Edie had put his long tail coat and red trousis under the bed.

'Allie's ma opens the winder to give him fresh hair. She sez, "Allie has etten something that doesn't agree with his bowilds. I'll give him a purgatory in the morning." When Allie's ma had gorn to bed, Allie slips out of the winder and puts on his black coat and red pants. Edie sez, if you doan come here and play the bend, I'll give you away and never forgive you.

'Allie orfs up the street to A H Williams and Co with jest enough time to get some boot pollidge on his face.

'I haven said all jest as it happen because you kep on inter-ruptioning me as you was talking. What I didden get from

Allie and Edie I got from the house mate Florestina, who is a
friend of mine.'

17

The Band in Action

My meetings with Christina had become more or less regular, either at my house or her cottage.

'I was telling you, Frenkie,' said Christina, 'that we salaged fort into the street with that feller Allie as conducer of the bend. We all parade, the main bory in the front, the sisters of mercy in the rear. Then that feller Allie gits us up into lind.

'Here was you all blackfaced in the front, don you rember? Behine was me with Rosaline holding up my train – not too high – then comes Johannes the tax collector. I tole Allie that before I done my dance he could interjuice me as Queen Jezebil or one of those English queens that wore trains.

'So off we went.

'I must tell you that James had got a letter from Mr John Truro Wild, the Magistrate, saying that yous could hold a Nigger Minstrel in the public thoroughfears and that you wuzzen to be interfear with. I seen that letter. James put in it a coupler odds and ens that Mr J T Wild must of forgotten. The letter was put in a big arnvelope.

'Well anyways, off we sets, Allie with his long knobkerrie in one hand and the big arnvelope in the other. Allie shouts, "Forward march in sex columbs of four and display to the right at the first street." (He was trying to immerate the Cape Infantry.) "First stop and halt," he says, "will be befour the sanitary of that noted rebel outlaw and distributor of peace,

Demmit."

'When we gets to Demmit's house, the lights was all out. He mus of known somethink. We starts out with soft music, like Swanny River and Poor Ole Joe.

' "Seems to me he's asleep," sez Harry, "let's wake him up." Harry goes to the back ranks and puts them in order, then he picks up a stone outer the street, flings it high and it drops a loud clunk on Demmit's tin roof.

'That wakes Demmit up and he comes out in a long night gownd. "I'll have the law on yew," he shouts, but before he could do his sez there was such a shower of crackits and squibs round him that he fleet into the house and bold the door.

'We gave him a farewell song that James tort us, it was somethink like this:

We'll hang old Demmit on the sour sycamore
If he doan git sick we'll hang him up some more
Till he's sick of the sycamore.

'Harry lets another stone drop on the tin roof of Demmit's house and we passes on peaceably up the street under the conduct of Allie.

'All the pibble seemed to know about this bend. Their doors were open and their lights were shining. We sang our songs at one house and another. Johannes's bolder hat got so full of cetsh that he couldn hardly put it on, I helped him.

'That night there was a dinner at the officers' nest of the Cape Infantry. Your three sisters wuz there. We went there and it being a military party we had to do things in stilde.

'Allie gets out his big arnvelope with the letter inside. "Surmount the troops," he sez to the stewart who comes out to see who was there. Then Allie does his reel stuff. He shouts out:

Oh yea! Oh yea! Oh yea!
All you loyal subjicss of Magistracy
Queen Victorious
Come out and do your duty.

'A Lieutenant in his red coat comes out to see, goes back in to report to the Colonel. By that time the bend was in full swing, singing a speshul song for the Colonel who was an Irishman. I forget the words but it was somethink about the wearing of the greend.

'"My Gord," says the Colonel, smoking his long seegar as he shows the ladies to seats on the veranda. "I never heard anything just like that outside Ireland."

'James had trained us well, speshally for the Colonel. Everyone liked him, he was a real gentleman.

'Anyway, the ladies and officers all settles down on the veranda listening to our conciet. When I comes on with my Spannidge prima donas dance, the officers laughed to bust their selves. It may of bin that Rosaline lift my skirts a bit high but I didden mean anything funny about it, so's to make pibble laugh.

'That was the end of the show there. When Johannes took his bolder hat roun it was nearly filt with money.

'We was going to our homes in good disorder, when one of yous sez, "Let's give Allie's ma and pa a treat."

'I said it woulden be safe, Allie's ma being that kind of persond.

'The next thing we was at Allie's house and Harry open the bend with his tin whistle. The house was in darknist. After a wild Allie's ma come out and says if we didden git orf at once she'd set the dorg on us.

'Nattie shouts out, "You havven got a dorg, only two rets and mangy at that, you is the third."

'Allie's ma looked that fierce. She had her hair all done up in curlers. She darts into the house, saying she was going to fetch the gun, but Allie's pa comes gives us half-er-crownd and says we better git away before the missis brought it. We went orf quietly.

'Meantime that clever girl Edie had got her brother out of the party, scrubbed the boot pollidge orf his face and put him in bed. "You jest keep on being sick with a sore head," she says. "I put your nigger close out of sight." Allie plays the part, he lays in bed groaning so loud that his ma come to see. "I think I had a bad nightmare," he says, "I thort I heard – a bunch of fiery fiends, singing songs, outside."

'"It's your bowilds," says Allie's ma, "I'll give you that purgatory in the morning."

'Allie says that he was feeling much better and didn need a purgatory, but she give it him early nex morning. You didden see Allie for a coupler days, he was away from school so he got his own back on the purgatory.

'That's the way the bend end.'

18

Jimmie Walsh

'I tole you all about the bend, but not quite all,' said Christina. 'There was one thing I forgot. That was Jimmie Walsh, and that spole the whole bend for me.

'This Jimmie Walsh just seem to have come from nowhere. He hedden no parings and no nothing. He used to help that strong man Plunket in the blacksmith's shop. He slep in a little room at the back of it and Plunket's father used to give him food. He wanted to be in that Nigger Bend, but he had no mothers or sisters to make the right close for him. He was at the back of the bend, singing sweeter than any of yous could.

'This Jimmie Walsh hadden even a hat, so you could see his hair the colour of gold, red gold.

'Jimmie used to go out by himself, when he wuzzen helping Plunket, and he used to sit and sing to himself. He had one shoot of close that he always wore. When the trousis wore out round the uncles, he cut them off to make them neater, but they wore out again and he kep on in this way till there was nothing lef to his trousis up to his knees. I doan know what they was like behine because when anyone come along Jimmie jes set down. When his work was done he wandered out in the veld and set, singing to himself, because he didden know anyone was listening.

'Jimmie was that shy about his worn out close that he wooden go to Billy Tyson's school. He jest helped Plunket in the blacksmith shop. And then in the afternoons when his work was done, he'd jest wander out into the veld and sing to himself.

'Then one day that big bully named Tom, you know who I mean, comes along and says you always singing or swinging or slinging, carnt you do something else, jeering like.

'Jimmie puts down his hammer, looks at Plunket who winks his eye and nods his head. "I'm not much good at singing so fur," says Jimmie, "but I got some idea of swinging."

'With that Jimmie ups and hits Tom one in the jaw. Me and Katrina seen and heard the hole thing, we jes happen to be on the spot.

'Jimmie picks up his hammer to go on with his job. "That's hard enough hittin for one day. Where you larnt this?" sez Plunket.

'"Oh, jes knocking around," says Jimmie. "It was either slinging or singing, otherwise I should of starve."

'"Well," says Plunket, "you tamed Tom and he needed it. The little boys were dead skeert of him, now they won't be if you about."

'James had give me ten bob out of the hat from the Nigger Band, he give Rosaline and Johannes five bob each. He said there was to be a commission meeting as to wot was to be done with the rest of the money.

'With my ten bob and some small chain in my pocket I was in the shop of A H Williams and Co on the day of the commission meeting. I buys a few peppermens, fingers a lot of things I didden want to buy and somehow gets near the door of James's office where the commission meeting was being held. The arge was what was to be done with the money. One says the money should be divide, equal sheet to sheet. Then one of yous says, "Wot about buying Jimmie Walsh an outfit of close?" There was a little silenst and then you all gits up and sings your navel anthem about Demmit and the sycamore. That mend that the proposal was carried unuproars.

'James disperges the meeting in disodour and fixes it. He sends for one of yous to fetch Jimmie Walsh.

'Jimmie come down by all the back streets. His close was that wornd out that they could hardly hide his personal properties. He slips into James's office.

'"What I done, Mr James?" he says, skeert like. James says he hedden done anything perticler, except his slosh on that bad bully feller Tom, and all the boys was giving him a present. James shows him all the new close laying on the table. "That's all yours," says James.

'Jimmie jumps up with his mouth wide open. "But they carnt!" says Jimmie, as he flops down in the chair, puts his two hands over his face and sobs and sobs. I could see the cheers trickling through his fingers and the sun shining from the window on his red head. I takes the stronges pinch out of my snuff-box I ever took.

'James pats Jimmie on the soldier and says, "This is a gif from your frens, partly because they likes you and partly because of your outing Tom."

'"That's differend," says Jimmie, "if I thort it was an ack of cheridy, I would of thrown this lot of close in the water furrer."

'"It's closing time," says James, "you better go home and take your things with you."

'I'd bort more peppermens that day than I could have eat in a week, but I got fax, which was the next maint thing.

'Jimmie gathers up the close in a bundle and orfs up a back street. I thort it would be nice to see Jimmie in his new close so I saunders up to Katrina's, the one that works for Plunket's ma.

'Katrina and me sets gossering for a bit, waiting to see

Jimmie come out of his room in his new close, but it wuzzen like that. He come out in his old regs, the trousis jes linkering above his knees. His face was whitern this tablecloth. Then he goes off hat foot into the veld.

'Katrina and me maunders orf in that direction. There was Jimmie setting on top of a high rock with his face between his hends. Then he stends up on top of that rock, flings out his arms wide, jest like a bird let out of a cage that was going to fly, and he begin to sing. Katrina and me maunders more slower so that we could year. We Griquas are fond of music. Me and Katrina sets down and swops snuff, making as if we hedden seen Jimmie. He hedden seen us. He first sings about a lark and then about a dove. That was jest right, his voice was as soft and sweet as that of any bird.

'Yes, Frenkie, it's only an old Griqua woman wots talking to you. But we has our inside feelings.

'Sudden, Jimmie sees us. He comes down with clinched fists. He curst us with words I never hear before. He said we'd been sprying on him. I saw it was the time for ackshun, so I jest sits still. "Where you come from, Jimmie?" I sez. "We was jest taking snuff. Carnt we take snuff without you disturving us with a convulshun? We didden know you was about."

'Jimmie seem satersfy. And with, "Sorry, Christina," he goes home.'

19

More about Jimmie Walsh

'Frenkie, this here Jimmie Walsh was a strange boy. He wudden wear those new close. One day when me and Katrina were gossering, his door was open. We saw him fingering those close as if they was something preshus and breakable like your ma's old chinda plates and cups.

'When he sees me and Katrina setting there, he turns white and clinges his fists. We took no noticed. Then he unclinges his fists. "You wait here a bit," he says, "and I'll show you something."

'He goes back in his room and after a wild he comes out with those new close on. They fitted him perfect. He takes orf his hat, bows and says: "To interjooce James Walsh. Tomorrow I goes to the Boys' Public House School."

'I knew then that Jimmie was on his feet, it was those new close done it. We admire the close and Jimmie was please but I warns him that a boy's firs day at school might be a bit hard. He sez that would be orl right.

'Nex morning I maunders down to the school early to see my fren Maria, who was Master Billy Tyson's cook. I wanted to burrow pattengs for a dress. The boys comes strangling along and plays in the yard. Then comes Jimmie in his noo shoot, the boys had been used to seeing him in rags. Then one of the big boys larfs out loud, points his finger and says, "Jest look at Jimmie." Jimmie, whose face gorn white, sez, "Jest have another look before you carnt look no more."

'With that Jimmie hits the big boy once, twice, then the school bell rings and you all goes into school – that is, except the big boy whose name was Bob, you know who I mean. Bob was washing his face in the water furrer trying to keep his eyes open, but he didden go to school that day. That's the way Jimmie started at the Public House School. It give him a sort of interduckshun and all the boys wanted to be his fren.

'So Jimmie begun a noo kind of life all because of the close you had give him. When he went home from school he took off his noo close, put on his ole ones and help Plunket in the blacksmith shop, but he still kep going out in the veld to sing.

'One day the boys at the school, while they was having their intervals, asked Jimmie to sing to them. He didden want to, but he takes a long breath and looks round. Then he swings his arms wide and sings. Yous Russians set still as dead mice. And then, when the song was over, you crep into school.

'Master Billy Tyson seen and heard all this and reports to the parson who wanted boys for his kwire. This parson was called Cannon, but he had nothing to do with the army.

'Jimmie was asked to join the kwire. He did, and they had a lot of practices. My friend Selina lived at the parsonage and I heard something from her. I went to church on a day she menshun. There was a coupler spews reserged for us collard pibble.

'I didn mind the sermint and the rest of the perceedings. I was waiting for the coral servist. I seen Jimmie in his white surplist, but he was jest joining in with his mates.

'Then Jimmie comes out from the bunch. The sun was shining on his head from a winder. He looked like a angel. I knew that he had jest that devil in him that would make him a reel good angel.

'Jimmie steps forward, folds his hands. The organ starts.

Jimmie lifts his head and sings. It was as if he didden see a sould in that whole church, jist as if he was standing on the rock in the veld. He sang, Inclinde thine Year, or something like that. It wuzzen the words I was listening to, it was the music.

'When Jimmie ended his song I slips out of the church, jist before the collecshern plate come roun. I took a whole lot of snuff to prove I hadden been crying.

'Anyways, I become a good Christian and went to church regular jest to hear Jimmie sing.'

20

Jimmie Again

'Now this here Jimmie Walsh done well in Billy Tyson's Public House School and everything seems to be going right with him. Then he goes and gets sick. Me and Katrina finds him rolling and tossing on his bed in the little room back of the blacksmith shop. He was as dry as a boand and hot as a stove. We makes a report to Plunket and he sends for the dockter.

'Plunket's ma was sick with another new baby or something and couldn help. She was that kine of woman – sort of useless. I think she'd hed too many babies from her youth up, starting with Plunket, there follows Nattie and Erbie and Billy and some others that doan matter.

'The dockter comes along and says Jimmie has got peumania and mus be taken to horspital at once. Jimmie hears the word horspital. That woke him up for a bit. He says, "To hell with a horspital if I gotter die I'll die jest here in a place I love."

'The dockter lifts his shoulders and sez, "What to do?" He lef some maracine, we give it to Jimmie. He falls nearly asleep.

'I tole Katrina to keep guard while I went to report to Frances. She comes down at once and between the three of us we kep watch on Jimmie. I think it was us being there, espesh-ally Frances, that kep Jimmie alive.

'Very early in the morning me and Frances gets up from watching, leaving Katrina in charge. As soon as we gets to the big house your ma calls for you. "Frenkie," she sez, "I want you to give me that young pet fowld of yours." You was fond of that fowld, where you got it I doan know, I never arsts questions like that, you might have stole it or it might have been given you.

'You runs to the fowl house and comes back with that pet fowld under your harm. You could do anything with that bird. When you come with that cockrild you looks fiercer en a wild cat. There was a good deal of talk. Frances was very patiend, explain that Jimmie was very sick and that if that fowld was made into soup, it might safe Jimmie's life.

'Then you does the only decen thing I ever seen you done in the whole of your disrispekable life. You hands over the fowld to your ma Frances and sez, "From me to Jimmie." And then you bolts up the backyard and climbs up to the top of the highes tree. You always done this when there was trouble about, if it was to get away from a hiding or you was otherwise unheppy. The thing I ken say as an hones woman is that you didden get nearly enough hidings. You used to come down orf that treetop as if nothing had happen and your parings had proberly forgot what you done.

'Anyway Frances an me gets busy with your fowld and puts it in a pot. She made chicken wrath as only she could make it. We takes the soup down to Jimmie's place and hots it up.

'Jimmie looked as if he was dead. But he was breathing. Frances puts her gentle hand behind his head and puts some of the soup in his mouth. Jimmie lays back on the pillers.

'After a while his lips start moving. He was trying to sing. There was no words, but by the way his lips move, I knew it was the song Inclinde thine Year. I goes outside and takes a couple er pinches er snuff.

'Frances give Jimmie a little of that soup every now en then. We sets on through the night. Then Jimmie hardly stops breathing. "This is the crisist," says Frances.

'Then, after a while, Jimmie settles down on his pillers and goes to sleep. This was very early in the morning. "He'll get better," says Frances.

'I goes outside and round the cornder out of earsight, lets up a coupler Hallelujahs and takes some snuff. If Frances says he was going to get better, he was. We always knew that what she said was true.

'We sets watching. The door was opent for air and jest as the sun was beginning to rise, Jimmie opens his eyes, stirs in his bed and looks out. His mouth was moving. There was no soun, but I knew he was wanting to sing the song about the lark.

'After some days Jimmie begun to recover by leaks and bouns. He was soon back in Billy Tyson's Public House School and back in the kwire in the church. Then I become a Christian for at lease the second time.'

21

And More Jimmie

'Jimmie went back to school and he sung in the kwire. He'd got sort of longer and bigger since his sickness, but nothing had damage his voice.

'Then going to church to hear Jimmie sing I seen a new feller in the kwire. He looked nice. He was setting nex to James of A H Williams and Co. When they finished with the sermint and all that kine of thing this new feller stands up. The orgint begins very soft and the feller begins to sing. It was so bootiful that I was jelles for our Jimmie. That bloke just sang as if the voist didden belong to him, as if it come from somewhere else, he sung jest as if he wuzzen trying.

'After a little wild, Jimmie gets up. He did wot he orten to of – not in church – he flings his harms wide. Then he foles his hends. The orgint begins so's you could hardly year it. Jimmie and the organeer had become frends and they'd hed a lot of practices, so they come to know each other well and their way of doing things.

'When the time come Jimmie lifts his face to the roof of the church and sings as if there wuzzen a sould in the place and as if he didden care if there wuz or wuzzen.

'When he finish his song, I slips out jest before the collecshint plate come round, I had to have some snuff. As I was going out of the vestuary I seen a little box, on it was write for the sick. I takes out the last half crownd I had lef over from the money

214

from the Nigger Bend. The church virgin had his back turn and nobiddy knows about that half crownd, except you whom I'm telling now. I needed that half crownd. Well anyway, I done it and so sits under that big hoax tree behine the church where I took quite a lot of snuff.

'Then out of the church comes James wot works for A H Williams and Co, the strange feller wot sung and Jimmie. They had taken their surplises orf and looked like ordinary pipple.

'I wuzzen listening much because I doan interfere with other pipple's affears, at lease not offen. There was some palarker.

'Then I years this: "Will you come with me, Jimmie?" from the strange feller, "I'll give you a charnst to do what I know you ken do – singing."

'Jimmie looks this feller up and downd, jest like that. "I think I likes you," he says. "I think I'll go with you, to sing."

'Then I takes a hend in the percession. I looks this gent up and downd jest as Jimmie done. You carnt do this on us, young man, I sez – Jimmie belongs to us. I was ready to skretch his hendsome face ter bits.

'James says, "Steady, Christina."

'The gent goes on: "I want to take Jimmie and hope to make him into a great and famas singer."

'I sez, Jimmie *is* greater and famasser than you can ever make him and he belongs to us. Everyone of us loves him for his deviltry, for his singing, for his bravery and – and jest because – because he's Jimmie.

'Jimmie says, "Shut up, Christina." It was like a clout in the eye.

'The gent goes on talking very quiet and then he says, "Come and listen to this, Christina." He opens the church door. The virgin and the organeer was still there, and nobiddy else. The gent goes up to the organeer and sez something, he

215

turns to Jimmie and sez something. Jimmie nods his head and I could see the shine in his eyes from where I was setting. I heard Jimmie say, "I know it, my mother taught me to sing it and we used to sing it together."

'The gent and Jimmie stands up together and the orgint begins. I didden think much of that song at its start, but later on the music so overrun me with its booty that I wanted to git up and smash all the furniture in the church.

'After the song the gent comes to me and says, "What did you think of that, Christina?"

'I says, May Gord blast you. There's nothing you can teach our Jimmie about singing. I'm going to report to Frances and have you put in jail for something.

'I darts out of the church. On the way up to the big house I had to see Maria and tell her the fax and I had to see Katrina and tell her all about it. Then I goes to the big house. I was all wroughten up and goes straight to the droring room.

'There sits Frances making tea with the gent!

' "What's it, Christina?" arsts Frances.

'That! I says, pointing at the gent. He wants to rob us. I was all heating up.

'Frances looks at me hard, tells me to go out and sez that she'd send for me later.

'Now I had moren a skint full for one day. I thort I'd go and heng myself, but coulden find a rope, anyway the tree was a bit high. Then I thort I'd drownd myself in the swimming poold. I rember that the swimming pools wuzzen very deep an I might get out, so I went to look for a big stone to tie roun my neck, I cooden fine a stone jest the right size. Having decide to put an end to my live, I felt much better. I was still serging for a stone the right size to keep me down underwater – stones was skeerge about there. While I was serging one of the maids comes up and sez the missis want to see me. So I had to put

216

the shooside off for a bit.

'I goes into the droring room and lifts my skirts at the sides and curtshies to Frances, who looks at me sort of cold. I does the same curtshie to the gent.

' "I want you to aperlegise to this gentleman for your rudeness," says Frances.

'I curtshies again and sez, Very sorry, sir, but I means it.

'The gent larfs sofly and I almost begun to like him.

'Then there's a knock at the door. In comes Jimmie. He bows to Frances, jest as a prince in the pitcher book might bow to a queen, and if there ever was a queen her name was Frances. He gives a nod to the gent. Frances takes him by the hand and kisses him. I could see him shiver. He takes her hand and kisses it.

' "This gentleman," says Frances, "is an old friend of ours and he wants to take you away singing. Can you sing?"

' "I try to, ma'am," says Jimmie.

'I was tole to call Miss Ketsie your sister and she and Jimmie goes into the big droring room. Miss Ketsie had been tole by the gent what to expec. She hits a note in the middle of the pihannah. Jimmie sings that note so's there was no difference. Then Miss Ketsie goes up and down the pihannah slowly. Jimmie goes up and down with his voist and there was no difference between him and the pihannah. Miss Ketsie arsts him to sing a song and gits out some music. She sez, "Do you know this, Jimmie?"

' "Yes," he sez, "I know Hark the Lark and I know the words."

'There wuz a big open winder there with a garden outside. The birds was twittering in the trees. As soon as Jimmie begun his song the birds all shet up en, Frenkie – you can believe it or not – those birds all came up to the neares trees to the winder and when Jimmie finish his song about the lark, those birds all

217

sings as I never heard birds sing before. Jimmie was a sort of magiciand with his voist. Miss Ketsie closes the pihannah very quiet, looks a long time at Jimmie and then disappears.

'I been sitting in the pessarge all this wild listening both ways. Frances calls me up and says that Jimmie was going away with the gent to sing. I hitches up my skirts at both sides and curteshies to the gent. I said to him very quiet, so'st Frances cooden year, May God blarst you for what you done on us.

'That afternoon Jimmie and me goes for a walk, though. As we were going along I sez, Jimmie, you come here like a lame lorst dorg, so Plunket's people took you in. Nobiddy knows nothing about who you wuz or where you come from.

'"I'll tell you, Christina," he says, "but if you pass it on, I'll take the skin off your hide, and you know I could do it.

'"My mother was a singer, a very beautiful lady. I got my singing from her. My father was a prize frightener and he tort me all I know about fighting. We used to have some jolly evenings. He'd get down on his knees so's to be level with me and show me jest how to hold my fists.

'"One evening my dad says to me, You got the idea, Jimmie, but you doan hit hard enough. Hit me as hard as you like anywhere you like. By that time I'd learnt most of his fighting tricks. I waits my charnst and with all my strength hits him a zonker on his chin. Sorry, sir, I sez.

'"I tort you all I knows, he sez, holding his handkercheff to his face, come and sing for your mother.

'"My mother died soon after that and my father drunk himself out. There was nothing. Pipple wanted to put me in a lorst home for orfings. I said I wuzzen lorst, I knew jest where I was and I refused to be an orfing. I didden want to be interfere with.

'"If these pipple come to look for me in the morning I doan

know, anyways I wuzzen there. I got together what food there was and a blankit and orf I went before dawn in the morning.

'"I gorn a long way when I come to a streamb. I had put a toweld and a bit of soap inside that blankit. When I gits to the streamb, I strips, gits in the water and washes, then rubs down with the toweld. My father tole me there was nothing bettern a rubdown after a tussle. Then I sings a coupler songs jest as nakend as I was. I never seng better. The streamb was the pihannah I had to keep in shune with it, the trees was there and some birds about. A little buck comes up very quietly. I went on singing, then some monkeys comes along on the treetops to year. That little buck licks me on the side of the laig. The monkeys comes down out the trees and I gives them some food."

'This is what Jimmie tole me, an I believe what he sed as certain as I believe in the Bible and hell and damnation, because Jimmie tole me. You see, I known Jimmie bettern the inside of an old coat and you boys didden know him hardly at all.

'Well, that's what Jimmie tole me. I can tell you all this now, Frenkie, and I'm sure Jimmie wooden mind – that was a long time ago and I kept my mouf shet about it all these years. I may not of tole you exac, for better or for words, what Jimmie said, but it's as near as I can rember.

'Jimmie made his way along. His food ran out. He had slep in the bush several nights. He turns up at a dorp nearly starving, goes to the hotel and sets down in the bar. The barman arsts what he wants. Jimmie says, faint like, "Something to eat." The barman looks at him hard and says, "We get lots of tramps calling in but none as young as you." The barman gets him some food.

'"Where you gwine?" arsts the barman. Jimmie, feeling better, says, "I'm just going on, thanks for the food."

' "Looking for a job?"

' "Yes," sez Jimmie, looking round the bar. "I'm one of the best bottle and glass washers in the country, brought up to the trade."

'You see, Jimmie had been brought up with acters and had a ready answer to anything. He washes glasses and bottles in that pub for a bit for his keep and a coupler bob a day. One day he hears two boys fighting in the street. He went out to have a see. He gets between those boys and sez, "I'm ringmaster and referee, you mustn't do it like that, you doan know the rules." The two boys looks at Jimmie in surprise and then they both sets on him. Jimmie flops them bofe out good and proper, went back into the bar and goes on washing glasses. The barman looks at him with his mouth open. "Neat work," he says, "I done a bit of fighting in my time, was tort by a man name Walsh. Wot's your name?"

'Jimmie goes on polidging a glass slowly, "My one name is Bendorf, the other is Couper."

' "Hell," says the barman, "you come from a big fighting straind on both sides."

'If the barman looked for Jimmie nex morning, Jimmie wuzzen there. He had lef some kind of a note of thanks to the barman. He was off on the road.

'I had all these fax in dribs and drabs from Jimmie. He come along in this direckshun, singing here and there and a little fight now and then to keep things heppy, as Jimmie put it.

'When he gets here, he's down and out. Plunket's people took him in.'

22

Jimmie's Farewell

'The day come for Jimmie to go away for his singing. The postcart used to start very earldy in the morning before it was proply light.

'I calls the other gels as a sort of depushun. We was there three hours before the postcart come up. I seen a light in the bar winder where that chap Alf, you know who I mean, was doing up luggage and stuff for the postcart. Knowing my way about, I goes round the back and gets into the bar. A coupler gins, Mr Alf, I says.

'"Bit early, aint it, Christina?" says Mr Alf. "Two gins – where's your friend?"

'I'm both here, I says.

'Alf gives me two gins. He tole me it was slow gin. I took his advist.

'When I got outside that bar in the col air, I reckon that Mr Alf's slow gin was about the quickes think I ever swaller. When I get round the cornder, here's the water furrer coming towards me. I coulden stop it, so I step in and sets down on the bank with my feet in the water. Then the other gels come up and arsts wot I was doing like that with my noo eleskit side boots on. I said it was these dam cornds that was paining me.

'The gels must of smell something one way or another. Anyway, they goes round the cornder where Mr Alf was. When they come back they was walking as if they had cornds all over their feet. I never sez anything bad about another womand, but it look to me as they been drinkin.

'By the time the postcart turn up all our cornds was better. We curtshies to the parson – the one they call Cannon and didn belong to the army. He come to say goodbye to Jimmie. A lot of you merchands was there and Plunket too. Then comes Billy Tyson, the master of the Public House School. Billy Tyson was all reformed and he comes limping up.

'So there was the parade. Jimmie with that gent comes out of the hotel. The parson says, "God bless you, Jimmie, you done more in my church that I could of in a long time." You merchands sings, "He's a jolly good feller" and Harry plays his tin floot.

'As Jimmie was just going to git in the cart Billy Tyson comes up, takes Jimmie's hand in both his crooked ones and says, "Good luck to you, Jimmie, here's something from me." I seen a purse pass from the crooked hands into the soft one.

'Jimmie and the gent gets in the cart. I goes on the fur side of the cart and says to the gent once more, May Gord blast you for what you done on us.

'He says, "Don't worry, Christina."

'I goes to the other side of the cart to say goodbye to Jimmie. "Thanks for all you done for me, Christina," he sez.

'I holes his hand and says, Sing for us, Jimmie.

'That swinde Christian the driver cracks his whip. Why he was call Christian I doan know.

'Jimmie waves his hand and starts to sing as the cart moves off. A sweetness comes to us through the early morning, then fades away.

'We gels went to see if Mr Alf was still there. He wos.'

Christina didn't tell me more of Jimmie Walsh then, but she showed me some picture postcards he had sent her. These she drew from a handkerchief tenderly, one by one. They indicated that he had sung with the greatest success in various cities. There was one of Jimmie walking in a garden with a lady who could only have been his mother's sister.

Christina always hoped that he would come back, but he didn't. James and I knew that Jimmie had died in Ireland. We couldn't tell her.

23

The Picnic

'I told you a lot of things about Jimmie Walsh,' said Christina. 'That was because, to me, he was the most wonderfulles boy in the whirl. He went away for other places and I may tell you something about him another time, but not now. I want a rest.

'Jimmie being gorn, I was able to pay more attention to you ruffiands.

'Johannes had long ago appolergise for pinching your father's apples and for the sploshing you give him one way and another for doing it. He was forgive. So he became a sort of head crook and bottle watcher to all of yous that was members of the roberts lair. He had to do jest what he was tole.

'Yous had a picknick every now and then. You was allowed to kill one fowld for raisins. This was all done in order. Yous parades at the woodpile and takes maggots of wood. Then you selex one fowld and that was the only one that was to be kilt, the others was free from interferange.

'This day I am telling you about there didden seem to be many fowlds around. Then a white one comes out from under a haige. You flings your maggots and kills the white fowld.

'Now this poor white hen had been setting on a clutcher of aigs. Off you goes on your picknick. I finds out about the misdreamer later. I went up to the fowld coop to look for a hen to put on those aigs. The only one I could find was black. She was clucking as if she wanted something. I ketches her and puts her on the nest under the haige. She settles down jest nice – jest what she wanted.

'When yous set off for that picknick, each of yous has a bag to carry the raisons. The eldes of you three had bread and butter in his and you has a bag with dates and other sweetmeats in – the lightest bag of the lot because you wos littler then the rest.

'Your middle brother had a bad cold and your ma Frances says that he mussen go to the picknick unless he wore her Scotch plate shawl to keep him warm. She was very fond of that plate. It was grey and white with some black. I knew it well and I often seen Frances throw it over her soldiers in a sort of grand way which show she was Scotch from where the plate come from. She didden do this on purpist, it was jest natrel.

'Anyways, you merchands goes off. Your eldes brother with the fowld in his bag, your middle brother with the plate all wrop round him and his bag with the bread under it, you with your bag with the dates and sweets and things. Knowing something I wooden arrange it like that. Nattie and Erbie and Billy with that nice feller Harry, your loafer's brother, was waiting for you at the gate. There the picknick starts. That's all I knows about it from inside in fashion. The res was tole me by Johannes who was your head firemaker and cook that day.

'He sez firs of all you said you was getting tired and you sets down to res. Yous two et some the dates in the bag. You kep on getting tired and when you gets to Fred's Bush where the picknick was to be there wuzzen many dates in the bag.

'Johannes done a cude thing knowing the dates would be arst about. He made a hole in the bottom of your bag.

'At the top of Fred's Bush there is a great big smooth round rock where the stream run over. This day it was cover with ice. That eldest brother of you three says, "Let's slide." He gets a branch of a bush, sets on it and goes swish over the ice down to the bottom of the rock. All you other fellers shoot.

'Johannes was busy cooking that fowld. He does it in our way, packs it in clay and puts it under the coalds.

'After a wild you all comes back from your sliding and felling hungry and wants to know how the fowld is getting on. Johannes says, it not nearly ready. Yous decides to have some dates to go on with. There was very few. There was quite a lot of palarker about that, then Johannes shows them the hole in the bag and says it was sprising that better bags wuzzen pervide for pipple going out to picknicks. You two thiefs got away with that.

'Yous kep on arsting Johannes if the fowld was ready and he kep on saying it wuzzen. Then one of yous said it mus be, kicks away the coalds and pulls out the fowld with a stick. The clay round it was hot as fire. Yous had to wait till it cool off a bit. Then the clay was broke, the fevvers come off with it, and there was the half cooked fowld ready for eating. One after another yous tried to get your teef into it but give it up. Johannes said, "I kep on toleing you it wuzzen ready."

'There was still quite a lot of food betweend yous, but that fowld had made the picknick a faildure, so you decides to go home.

'On the way you comes to a place where the stream goes down a hole in the groun. One of yous says lets get in and see where it come out. In you goes one after another, excep Johannes who said he wuzzen going to hell that way, not at presint. By a mirrigle yous all come out at the other end, covered in mud but quite pleased with yourselfs. Then you strangles on the way home. All this is what Johannes tole me. You was all sworn to secret about going down that hole.

'On these picknick days I always kep a watch for yous coming home. I could count yous as you come down the hill so's to be sure there wasn gwine to be an inkwist on one of your dead bodies. I stands at the cornder of the fence and nearly fell dead when I seen what you looked like – all covered in mud, no seats to your pents. (Johannes explain to me afterwards this come from the sliding over the rock while he was cooking the hen.)

'I get you three and says in the fiercest voice, Yous come with me, you other scullions go home and get what's coming to you. I takes you three down to the swimming pool, under arres so to speak, and orders you to get in, wash yourselves and wait till I come back. I cuts a long switch off the quince haige to show you I mean what I say.

'I went to report to Frances that you was all back safe and soun, but that you was a bit dirty and I had tole you to have a barth. I gets some clean close out and goes back to the swimming pool and you puts them on. It was supper time and you three brothers setting at the table as hengry as rats.

'Your ma comes in and says, "Have you had a good day, boys?"

'You, Frenkie, being a talkertif sort of chep, sets out to tell about it, but when you comes to parts like sliding down the stone and going down the hole your brothers oldern you digs you in the rips and you shets up and gets on with your supper.

'Then your ma arsts your middle brother where he had put the plate shawl when he come back. His face goes as long as a horse and he says, "Sorry ma, I ferget all about it. I mus have lef it on the mountain."

'Your ma looks sternd, the only time I seen her look jest like that. "You and Johannes will go to the mountain tomorrow and bring back that plate," she sez.

' "Yes ma," sez your middle brother.

'Your middle brother and Johannes goes up nex morning to

find the plate shawl. They find it orrite but it was burnt almost to bits. The fire where Johannes been cookin that fowld had spead a bit after you left and had got the shawld. It wuzzen Johannes's fauld.

'Your middle brother gethers what was lef of the shawld and carries it down the mountain. They gets to the big house and your middle brother goes to your ma with the burnt up stuff in his two hends and holds it out to her. She looks at him in a way that to him was worst then any punnigement. I was there then and saw this. There was no words.

'Frenkie, there must of been something about that plate shawld we didden know about, your ma was that sad.

'The only good thing that come out of that picknick was this. Frances your ma went to see how the hen under the haige was getting on with her aigs. There was a black hen with a bunch of white chickens. Frances says she was quite sure it was a white hen that bin setting there. I said it might of bin, but with a change of weather hens was lible to change their colour jus like a camiliond, I seen it happen to my father's fowlds.

'Frances may have felt there was something behine this, but I didden give you personages away for killing that white setting hen that you cooked and cudden eat.

'I spent that night putting petches in the seats of your pents you wore out sliding over that rock. I wuzzen particler about the colours.'

24

Odds and Ends

'Here's a coupler things I'd like to tell you, Frenkie,' said Christina. 'You was sometimes an abshloot curze to your two brothers oldern not much bettern you, excep the middle one who, wild he was differend to Jimmie Walsh, he was nearly as good. He never done a quarreld with other boys.

'You and he goes up, one day, to the Bangle Bush. It was call the Bangle Bush because one of your sisters lorse a bangle there, given to her by one of her cortshers. You went up to the bush to get some green stuff to decorate the schoolroom where there was to be a Bend of Hope – not like ours. There was some other kind of persond to speak to the young pibble.

'Anyhow, you and your middle brother gits the greens from the Bangle Bush and on the way home a cow spots the green stuff you was carrying and thinking it was something to eat follers you up. You yells out that a wild bull was chasing yous. You check down your green stuff and runs for the sod wall at the cornder where Mordie and me was looking out. Your middle brother also thort it was a wild bull, but he picks up the greens you thrown down and keeps well between you and the cow so that he get poke fust. You both gets over the wall, greens and all. That the kine of feller your middle brother was, protecking you like that.

'Well, you merchands puts that green stuff all round the schoolroom. Then there was a rival meeting with lots of

Halleluyers. Afterwids there was a meeting for the young pibble. This was a meeting for Goodtumblers. Yous children all promise never to git drunk and was all given a blue ribbond to prove it. That was a long time ago, Frenkie, and you may have lose that blue ribbond.

'Why I say you was a curze to your two brothers was that you wanted to go wherever they went and do what they do. I think you must of bin a bit of a nuisints.

'One day the boys gather, including Nattie and Erbie and Billy. There was some game on. They wanted to leaf you out as being too little, but you wuzzen takent anything like that. One merchant says, "Let's go to the museum." This was a back room on the outside of the big house and one of the stinkiest plazes I ever smelt. There was stuft birds – what you called stuft – bad eggs, worse lizards an wot not.

'You all goes into the museum – you in front, of course – and starts looking at the stinks. The nex thing is all the boys darts out of the door and locks it. Only Harry who plays the floot is left with you. He tries to get out the winder. You grabs him by the laig. There's a mew an cry from outside: "Let go, let go, his laig is coming off." You lets Harry drop, and orf they goes somewhere hate foot.

'Then you starts noises, shouting and banging the door. You gets over the wust and starts playing with the stinks. Your sisters and their cortshers hearing the noise come along and open the door. They was jes coming in. You sez, "Sixpence admishun to the museum, children half prized." Those three cortshers paid their sixpences so as to stay out. Your sisters told you afterwards you done a nasty thing on their cortshers and they was a bit fade up. They come and put a lot of dip in the museum.

'When the other scullions come back you shows them your three sixpences and they was a bit fade up and sez it wasn't your museum and how could you let pibble in without arsting. You says you hedden let pibble in, you had got sixpences for keeping the cortshers out. Besize, you say, you bin lef in char of the museum.

'It turns up later that your two brothers and the other scavengers had been to the field below the big house where old Paulse used to graze his donkeys. They made a cirkist out of those donkeys and didden want to take you for fear your neck would get broke as usual.

'Old Paulse tole me he cudden make it out, his donkeys was that tired one day he cudden get no work outer them. I didden tole him about the cirkist.

'There was one thing, Frenkie, I was always a little sorry about. Yous threes had to walk a mild to school. Your boots was what was called bluechers, they was hard and heavy. There was nothing blue about them and they was sort of barstard between boots and shoes, real ugly.

'Your loafer Mordie says one day, "What funny boots you got on."

'You get in a rage about that and kicks your boots on stones so they soon get wore out. You and your middle brother and me was sent down to old Hall's shop at the cornder to git you a new pair of boots. When we get to the shop, old Hall was serving another person who said he wanted size number three. This old Hall was always making poultry. He sez,

It is wonderful to me
That a long kêrel like ye
Can vat number three.

'You tries on boots and tries on boots – too big, too small, and then you goes to the shop winder and picks up a pair of eleskit side boots and tries them on. Your middle brother says

231

he duzzen like them, I say I didden like them, but you did, so the arge ended. You kep those eleskit side boots on and I kerry your ole ones. As you went up the street you coulden keep your eyes orf your feet, watching the tassils in front of those boots swinging. When you gets home you goes into the droring room where your sisters wuz. You sits down and stretches out your feet.

'When your sisters seen those eleskit sides, they first looks a bit shock. When you gits up and makes the tassils wobble they laughs to bust. You thought you done something smart with your noo boots.

'That was the day for Mordie's music lessent. You was waiting at the gate, boots and orl. Mordie comes up. You takes her hand and yous two walks down, your boots' tassils wobbling, but she didden notice. Then you sets down behind that rose haige. Mordie takes off her big hat and throws it on the grass. You was getting a bit impadiend because Mordie hedden notice your boots, so you stick out your feet and shakes them about. Mordie jest points, and then rolls on the grass larfing. "Wimmens' boots" was all she could say.

'Your engagement to Mordie was broke off for at lease a week from those boots, but I made it up between yous somehow. When your ole boots come back mend and clean they didden look so bad. Those eleskit sides somehow got lorse. I notice you had a noo catterpurl about that time, but I sez nothing. I foun one of those boots, but there was no eleskit in the sides.

'There was a lot of things heppen in those days, Frenkie. Some I seen, some you tole me about. And I hear a lot from the other gels.'

25

Goodbye

'Then come the time,' said Christina, 'when we was tole that your pa and ma and all of yous was going away. We coulden bear it. We was all jest mad and sad by turns.

'We didden see very much of your pa, he was often away stopping Kaffir Wars, which he done by himself. When he rides down the street on that chestnit horse with a white face, name Manel, the women curtshies and the men lifts their hets. He would sometimes pull up and say a word to this one or that one.

'But your ma, Frenkie – your ma – wherever there was a sicknest or trouble whether it was in a big house or a tumbledown cottage, she was there. She heal the sick jest by being there, an she straighten out troubles jes by being there. There was something about her that was like a mirrigle in the scripshers.

'On a day the Cape Infantry parades. They comes down the street in their red coats, the bend in front, bugles blowing, drums ratterling. They halts and draws up in the square. Then your pa on a big yaller horse with a red coat officer behine rides up. The Cape Infantry gets an order and claps their hands on their guns.

'Your pa gets orf that yaller horse and he walks up and down the rangs with the red coat behind him. The bugles and drums starts again. After that your pa walks out with the Colonel and stands under the long pole where Queen Victory's fleg was flaying.

'Then the Colonel in a loud voice says: "I am instruct by her Magistracy the Queen to convey on you the Order of Seemjee, for honable, valable and faceful servige." The Colonel pins a medal on your pa's coat.

'After that the Cape Infantry fires a furious war three times. It was so loud I fell backwards from pastorage William Dower's mud wall where I been watching proceedens.

'I was feeling that weak, I went to look for the other gels. I found them. They said they was feeling weakern me. We went round that same cornder. Mr Alf was there. After a wild we feel a bit better and got home, having said goodbye to Sir Charles and Lady Frances. So those beloved people went away from us.

'Anyways … You being back with us, Frenkie, is somethink. But not much so far.'

Kokstad's Griqua Church and Manse fortified during the Basuto Rebellion of 1880, as illustrated by *The Graphic*

The handwritten original of *Cattle Thief*, with the typescript of it submitted by the author's agent A P Watt, together with a carbon copy from which the novel was typeset without cuts or rephrasings, was deposited by Frank Brownlee in the Harold Strange Africana section of the Johannesburg Public Library shortly after World War Two. The only surviving typescript of *Chats with Christina* is held in the National English Literary Museum, Grahamstown, together with much other material entrusted to them for safekeeping by his son. The East Griqualand Museum in Kokstad, a few blocks down from Brownlee Street at 98 Main Street, has background displays of both works.